Surfacing

A Global Paranormal Security Agency Story

Jodi Kendrick

SoulGate Publishing

JODI KENDRICK

Romance. Adventure. Passion.

Dragon Island
Dragon Heat

Enchanted Ardor
Wish

EveL Worlds : FUCN'A
Tough Nut
Diamond in the Ruff
Honeyed Nut
Gorilla in the Hiss
FUCN'A Collection One
Pedigree Collection

Finely Aged
Dragon Steel

Global Paranormal Security Agency
Awakened
Surfacing
Polestar
Aquatic Investigations
Prowler

The Kindred Chronicles
Healer
Mercenary

The Soaring Dragon Chronicles
Return Flight
Changeling

The Global Paranormal Security Agency

The Global Paranormal Security Agency is a hidden investigative group dedicated to bridging the paranormal and human worlds to keep everyone safe.

Protect. Defend. Seek Justice.

Thank you!

To my family, friends and writing community. Your continued love, support and encouragement keep me going. Without you, I'd still be dabbling and drifting.

Jessica Ripley – So many projects to keep me out of trouble!

To **Milly Taiden** – my deep appreciation for her generosity in opening her creative worlds to those of us that enjoyed playing in them.

For *my* grumpy Scot.

ONE

RAYA BURNS HOVERED IN the corner of the prison cell, staring at the scruffy, snoring inmate on the lower bunk.

She sighed.

It was time. It had been a long, unpleasant process, but she had a job to do.

Ignoring the second inmate, in the upper bunk, she floated closer, whispering close to his ear.

"Chuck, let's go."

Chuck flipped over, eyes wide, searching for the source of the voice in the dark. "Ashray?"

Who else would it be, after all these weeks of nocturnal visits to guide the prisoner in the process toward escape? She rolled her incorporeal eyes. "Yes, Chuck."

"We're doing this now?"

Seriously? "Yes, Chuck."

"Whoa, okay," He rubbed his eyes and scrambled out of the bunk, mindful of his neighbors hearing, and shoved his bunk mate, "Glenn."

As much as she disliked the excess baggage, it couldn't be helped. Since the cells were occupied in pairs, any activity couldn't be hidden. They'd ditch him later. For now, they had to focus on this particular step: Getting the hell out.

The second inmate grumbled, rolling over to see what Chuck wanted. There was a whispered exchange as he jumped down.

"We don't have time for this," she said to Chuck.

Glenn's eyes swept the small space as Chuck's had. She was used to this. They couldn't really see her as she was. If they bothered to focus hard enough, they might catch a wavering shape where her voice was.

"If we get caught, I'll shank you myself," Glenn snarled in Chuck's face. "Crazy fuck."

"Stay here then, just help me move the bed and I'll be on my way."

"I'm not fucking staying here to take the heat of your escape."

"Whatever man, just get moving."

Raya suppressed her impatience, ignoring Glenn's visible and offensive body ink—speaking of shanking....

The two men eased the bunk bed aside with practiced silence to expose the crude hole in the concrete.

She was grateful Chuck had been imprisoned in this old crumbling prison, and not in one of the shiny new super max facilities. It had been a challenge convincing Chuck to wait for her to guide them out, insisting she needed to get the escape route and supplies finalized. It was his problem getting Glenn to follow along.

She didn't think it was really all that hard. Despite his bravado, the loser was a coward and wouldn't have gone alone, anyway. They followed the sound of her voice as she led them along the old lead pipes and climbed the pipe braces she'd bolstered, up to the top floor. Then they moved through further breaks in the walls and along a ventilation shaft. Chuck had dropped a few pounds over the last few weeks in order to fit. She hoped Glenn's bony knees and elbows banging against the pipes and shaft walls wouldn't alert the guards.

Emerging from the ventilator shaft, they waited. Watching the guards, she instructed them on when to move and when to hold until they reached the edge of the roof top.

As they scurried across, the tower guard turned in their direction. "Get down," she commanded. Glenn dropped and Chuck stumbled toward the edge of the roof, losing his footing. She watched as he stumbled over the edge.

Oh, Christ.

Chuck's fingers clutched the ledge as Glenn stared at them from the shadows.

"If he dies, you're caught," she snapped, motivating him to help Chuck not die.

As the men struggled, with muffled grunts and scraping, she watched the guards.

They'd been heard.

One was on the radio and the two patrolling below them looked up as Chuck's feet disappeared from their line of sight.

"We don't have long." With the guards' attention turned toward the rooftop, they had to move carefully toward the smokestack at the opposite end of the building.

"Hurry."

The men moved as fast as they could without falling, scurrying down the crease between the stack and the wall. She led them along the water tower supports toward freedom, just beyond the gap she'd made in the fence surrounding the prison property.

The alarm went up as Glenn shimmied through the hole after them, crying out as he gouged knees and elbows on sharp stones in his haste.

Raya didn't stop moving, instructing Chuck as they went, scrambling toward the river.

Every bit of her stretched for it. For the safety and power of the water.

"Into the river."

They still couldn't see her clearly. As close as they were to the power of the flowing river and under the light of the moon, she knew she'd be more visible.

Glenn hesitated as he bypassed her. "What the fuck are you?"

"She's our angel of freedom," Chuck said.

There was barking in the distance as spotlights began to sweep the prison grounds.

"Get in the water."

"Fuck that, I'm going for the woods," Glenn said.

She considered letting him go as a diversion, as Chuck splashed into the water. An instant later Chuck's clothes floated, loose and shapeless. A thin translucent line whipped out of the water, striking Glenn across the exposed flesh of his throat, and disappeared again.

"What the fuck was that?" his hand reached for his throat, "Fuck, something is burning my neck, man." He glanced up, searching the bank, seeing that he was alone. "Chuck?"

"He's in the water, like you should be."

The barking grew closer.

Raya watched the wound turn red.

Glenn stumbled as he moved away from the river, tripping as he made his way toward the woods.

Glancing in Chuck's direction, she saw the inflated purple-blue bladder of a Man-O-War jellyfish floating among the prison garb.

Huh.

I guess he was tired of his cell mate.

She'd been curious to know if he was a shifter—and if so, what kind.

She had no idea how the fresh river water would affect him, and wouldn't have cared much if it weren't for the fact she had been hired to get him safely to his uncle.

She stepped into the water, unaffected by his long poisonous tentacles in her present state.

"There's a cache of civilian clothes upriver." She slid through the water. A moment later, he angled his fin and followed, leaving the prison rags as they were.

The frantic barking had reached the bank behind them.

TWO

IAN MCLACHLAN STEPPED OUT of the close walls of the elevator and drew a deep breath, adjusting his backpack on his shoulder. He searched the sign on the opposite wall, suppressing a yawn after a long night traveling; all the way from his lake home in British Columbia to New York.

It had been years since he'd stepped into the offices of the Global Paranormal Security Agency, and he hadn't expected to do so again. Ever.

But, Carson Perenga had called. And Ian owed him. It didn't matter how late—or early—it was.

A smiling assistant led him to Jack Maeda's office.

"I might be able to pull Teddy in, if you need him. Willow and Risa have gone to Antarctica with another unit, and everyone else is already out on assignment, so I want you to pull together your own team for this." Maeda was saying to Carson, frowning at his laptop screen.

"Already started," Carson said, as he glanced up at Ian's arrival and grinned.

"Good. I can't seem to find the file in the database. Ask Analiese Ortega to send it again." Finally noticing Ian's arrival, he turned his attention to him with a level gaze. "Well, look at who's risen from the depths of Loch Ness—or is it Okanagan these days? McLachlan."

"Maeda. Okanagan." He acknowledged and corrected.

The men stared at each other another moment longer.

"Well, now that we have that warm reunion out of the way, how about we get started with the meeting?" Carson said as he moved toward Ian, hand extended.

Ian took it and Carson pulled him into a bro-hug.

"Good to see you, old friend."

"It's been too long, man," Carson said with a hearty slap on the back before offering him one of the chairs facing Maeda.

Ian stood before Maeda, offering a hand across his desk.

Maeda slowly reached out and shook it.

Ian didn't miss the confusion that flashed across Maeda's face.

"You mentioned you need help with a case?" Ian said to Carson as he took the empty seat, dropping his bag next to it.

Carson nodded and leaned on the edge of Maeda's desk. "A while back, we broke a human trafficking ring on the west coast. Folks were being nabbed and moved to a ship sailing along the coast."

Ian nodded. The case had been all over the news. He glanced at Carson, if the GPSA was involved, then paranormals somehow were, too.

Carson went on. "Last night, one of the guys that worked on that ship escaped the east coast prison he'd been transferred to—some kind of agreement to be closer to family."

"He wasn't in a GPSA prison?"

"As far as we knew, everyone on that ship was human, if this guy isn't human, we're not sure what he is yet."

"So... Where do I come into this?" He checked his watch, suppressing another yawn, "at the ungodly hour of 7:30am?"

Maeda quirked a thick brow, grunting. "Carson let you sleep?" He grunted.

"GPSA was called because his escape seemed paranormal, according to the very few pieces of evidence collected. I called you in because you know the waters in that area better than anyone."

Ian nodded. He had split his time between a few different lakes in North America since he had left his ancestral home in Scotland.

"Alright, let me have a look at the particulars and I'll get started. Keep in mind, when I'm in this part of the country, I spend most of my time up at Lake Champlain, not on the coast."

Carson checked his phone, "Ana sent the files, Jack."

Maeda turned back to his computer, and a moment later the printer geared up. Carson brought the sheets back to Maeda's desk, and Ian stood to get a better look at what they were dealing with as Carson spread them across the desktop. There was a long report from Carson's human trafficking case that the prisoner was apprehended from. He'd read that later; for now, he looked at the images.

Mugs shots of two prisoners; Charles 'Chuck' Meduse and Glenn Smith, cell mates. Chuck was so unremarkable it was easy to see how he had been overlooked. The other guy was scrawny and covered in crappy tattoos, most of which were swastikas and other wannabe skinhead symbols and slogans.

Carson leaned over, pointing to him. "This one was caught in the woods in a bad state."

Ian looked up. "His cell mate tried to kill him?"

Carson shrugged. "He was found barely conscious from jellyfish stings across his throat, and muttering about ghosts."

"Jellyfish stings?"

Carson fished through the printouts still on the desk and handed one to Ian showing the reddened, whip-like marks seared into the flesh of the inmate's throat. "Looks nasty."

"The other guy hasn't been found. Just his clothes were retrieved from the river. Local forces don't know what to make of it."

"No doubt. What else do we know about the escapee?"

"Not much. Foreigner, from Canada. No priors, at least not here. Other inmates and prison guards aren't sure if he's deeply spiritual or needing medication of some kind. For months he's been witnessed talking to himself-or to someone no one else can see."

"Not his cell mate?"

Carson shook his head. "Talks more when he's alone, and usually at night."

"Psychic?"

"Maybe?" Carson checked his watch, "Ana's flight will arrive in another couple of hours."

"You're pulling her in from her post?" Maeda looked surprised.

Carson nodded. "As you said, everyone else is on assignment, and we work well together. Freddy is covering the office in her absence."

Maeda nodded.

"In the meantime, I'll catch Ian up to date on the original case over breakfast, then get packed for the drive once Lirikai brings Ana back from the airport."

"Lirikai?" Ian asked.

"Long story. Breakfast. Maeda, you coming with us? Breakfast is on you."

"Cheap old man." Maeda muttered. "Nah, I've got too much work to do. Carson, remember to grab some topographical maps and waterways charts."

Ian approached Maeda's desk and held out his hand again. "I've decided to start letting go of grudges," he said.

Maeda nodded, "Life is too long—much too long—for us to hold grudges, anyway. It's good to see you." He smiled.

"You still owe me fifty quid." Ian said, retrieving his bag.

"Jesus, Ian, that was decades ago. And didn't you just say you're letting go of grudges?"

"Grudges, not debts."

Maeda pulled his wallet from his pocket, "What's the exchange rate?"

"Interest too."

"What? It's been decades."

He tried not to laugh at the exasperation in Maeda's expression.

"Aye."

He grumbled, putting his wallet away. "None of that was my fault. Not really."

"You two can catch up over breakfast." Carson insisted, waving at the stack of case file sheets.

"I've got a sudden case of indigestion." Maeda growled.

Ian snorted. "Americans."

Carson and Ian rode the elevator down to the lobby and headed for Carson's favorite local diner. That was something Ian could always count on; Carson's ability to find all the best food joints, whether they were dives or five-star galas.

THREE

RAYA STOOD ON THE western bank of the Hudson River, waiting for Chuck, who was in the bushes, changing into the clothes she had given him from her cached pack.

So far, things were going well. "Come on, they haven't found us yet, let's keep it that way."

She hoped the authorities would focus on the coast or the city. She had been hired to get Chuck to Montreal, so that's what she was going to do. The easy escape route would have been to grab a boat and go up the coast. This way was much harder. It was vital for Chuck to remain hidden, because she desperately needed this job.

They were moving on foot, heading north, with very little sleep.

Chuck adjusted the sleeves that hung beyond his finger-tips. "My uncle will be in Montreal when we get there?" His features were strained.

She shrugged, "I'm supposed to get you there, I don't know who's going to meet us, yet." She considered him a moment, "Don't like that particular city?" she smirked.

"Nothing wrong with Montreal. Would have been easier going south." He glanced at her then away again.

She couldn't argue that. He wasn't alone in wishing they could take another route. She started walking, and Chuck fell in behind her.

THE DINER'S CONSTANT FLOW of customers, voices and clattering dishes had long faded to the background for the two agents.

Drinking his coffee, Ian ignored the human movement while Carson checked his phone.

"They're just leaving the airport, we can meet them at the hotel."

Ian nodded. "Good, my arse is going numb."

They'd gone over Carson's file, then he had caught Ian up on events related to the report. And on his new companion.

Ian was glad his old friend had found someone special, even if it was over a serial murder investigation. He was looking forward to meeting Lirikai. Barra'kidai were legendary even in the paranormal world. Ancient avengers created by the goddess of the oceans to detect, seek out, and destroy the filth of the world. The same goddess that had created his old friend Carson.

Carson flagged the waitress for the bill.

Ian smiled up at her as she flirted with him while Carson was distracted. She was very attractive, reminding him of another woman with smooth sun-kissed skin and thick curly black hair. A woman with a sensual smile and mischievous sparkle in her eyes. He left a generous tip on the table, grabbed his bag from the seat next to him and followed Carson.

They stepped out into the wall of noise of the awakened city. Drawing a deep breath, he fell in step with Carson.

"How long were you out at Okanagan?"

"Probably too long."

Carson nodded. "The city noise and energy are a bit of a shock to the system until it settles under your skin."

"I'm already missing the muffled world of the lake."

They wove their way along the sidewalks, crowded with all manner of people. Businessmen and women, street vendors and entertainers, hawkers and tourists. It was the same in every large city, but every city also had a distinct vibe to it.

In sharp contrast, on entering the hotel, Ian's head buzzed from the sudden lack of noise.

Carson glanced at him as they stepped into the elevator and grinned, "Lirikai doesn't like elevators either."

"Glad we have something besides you in common." His fingers gripped the strap of his backpack. The doors slid open and Ian drew in a breath. "I hate these things."

They collected Carson and Lirikai's belongings and went back down to the lobby.

Carson checked his phone, "They're just about here," he said, stepping outside as an SUV swung into the empty spot just in front of them. The trunk popped open before the vehicle finished rocking in place.

"Did you hire a stunt driver?" Ian asked, hauling the baggage into the open hatch.

Carson grinned.

A petite woman jumped out of the passenger side, her face devoid of color.

"Good to see you, Ana," Carson said, "This is Ian."

She glanced in Ian's direction, shot a hand out to shake, while her face stayed trained on Carson, voice tight. "You should have warned me that you taught Lirikai how to drive."

"She wanted to surprise you."

A nervous laugh escaped her. "Surprised!" She darted into the safety of the back seat, immediately strapping herself in.

An elegant hand patted the vacated front seat. "Carson, let's go, before lunch rush hour starts."

Ian got into the back seat next to Ana and strapped in. He looked up from the buckle to eyes trained on him from the driver seat. Lirikai was striking, and a little unnerving as the edges of her nostrils twitched. Seemingly satisfied, she reached back a hand, which he shook. Then she was all business again, chattering to Carson about the traffic.

Ana's hand reached for the handle bolted to the ceiling.

Ian's shoulder hit the door as the SUV darted into the line of traffic to a chorus of horns.

Ian glanced in Ana's direction. Her eyes were closed, lips moving. He thought he heard a whispered string of prayers coming from her lips.

By the time they reached the prison, Ian was just about ready for the safety of a lake. Any lake.

They met with the warden and reviewed the materials already in the file, along with the surveillance footage they'd retrieved in the ensuing hours. Interview transcripts were added to the file, which Ana quickly went through.

"Warden, I'd like access to the inmate's cell."

The Warden frowned, shaking his head.

To Carson she said, "I need to try to get a reading on what we're dealing with."

Carson glanced at Lirikai, his expression worried at the strain evident in her tight face and posture. They had argued back and forth at her refusal to wait in the car, but she had ended up coming in.

"Ian, will you go with Ana? It's too dangerous to even think about letting Lirikai go in there. She might lose control and we'd have a bigger mess on our hands."

"Of course."

After a few more minutes debating with the Warden, he agreed to let them in.

"Lirikai and I will be here, reviewing the security footage. Make sure Ana gets all the time she needs in that cell."

Ian nodded and followed Ana and the guard out of the office, through a series of security doors toward the main prison building.

The walls were a putrid green, while the floor tiles were so scuffed and time worn it was impossible to tell if they had ever held a pattern other than dirt skids. He focused on the doors. Thick steel doors, painted and repainted, older layers creating a topographical surface beneath the paint. They walked single file, a guard leading and a guard bringing up the rear of their little line, through the close confines of the narrow corridors until they reached the cavernous maw of the main cell block, rimmed with steel balconies and rows of barred doors holding back the inmates.

In front of him, Ana's hands curled into tight fists pressed against her thighs and her slender shoulders straightened. As soon as they stepped into view of the first cells the heckling started, mostly directed at Ana, some at the guards and some at Ian. It all went ignored. He could see the tension in his new colleague.

Up a single flight of stairs and three quarters of the way along, they stopped at a cell identical to all the others with the exception of its glaring vacancy. The guard opened it and stepped back.

Ana drew a breath and crossed the threshold, Ian a step behind.

The bunk bed was displaced from the wall, exposing the rough rectangular gap, excavated just enough to allow a man to get through. He wondered how long it had taken them to do it.

He could tell Ana was trying to focus, block out the voices and words echoing through the building toward them as her eyes slid around the sparse, yet cramped, space.

Ian stood sentinel, straight and tall, as though he could prevent the noise from reaching her.

Ana looked up at him, searched his face, her expression eased a fraction, "Please step out." When he opened his mouth to debate, she said, "I'll work faster if you do that."

Unable to argue, he stepped back out onto the grated balcony. He remained as he was, filling the space of the open door. The gathering tension eased. He centered his attention on what Ana was doing, while the guards waited to either side of the cell, curiosity evident as they cast glances in her direction.

After looking at every inch of the cell, she began to place her hand, palm down, on different surfaces. Then she picked up and cradled various mundane objects in her hands, eyes closed.

"What is she, some kind of psychic?" A guard asked, his expression dubious.

Ian shrugged, "Something like that." He really wasn't sure. Carson hadn't given him much detail about Ana.

The guard grunted and said nothing more.

She asked the guards several questions regarding the ownership of the sleeping spaces and level of disturbance of the room since their escape.

Crouching beside the lower bunk, hands out, eyes closed, she remained still for long moments. Moving to the tiny sink, her fingers drifted over other things as she looked around the space, below the bed and along the ceiling.

Ian hadn't expected her to bend down to the crude hole in the wall and slip through. He wasn't sure he could squeeze through after her.

"Ana?" He moved to step into the cell. She held up a hand, staying him.

The guards' attention was on the population behind their cell doors, protesting the unscheduled confinement during their apparent free roam time. Their frustrations were rising, the shouts more aggressive.

Ana reappeared, brushing the dust from her hands and jacket. "Let's go."

He stepped out and away, allowing her to exit. The guards wasted no time leading them back to the warden's office.

"Did you get what we need?" Carson asked Ana as soon as they returned.

She nodded.

There were more folders stacked with their original case file, and a thumb drive.

Carson spoke with the Warden a few moments, shook his hand, and the group were led back out to the public space of the building to retrieve their secured belongings.

There was a separate group of guards waiting to take them across the compound to the point of escape, explaining the suspected route.

They went through the break in the property's fence, down to the river where the inmate's clothes had been retrieved from the river, and the other escapee apprehended in the forest.

None of them spoke about the case in front of the guards, only asking questions where clarification was needed.

Once back in the quiet confines of the SUV, Lirikai started the vehicle. Ana directed her to drive north while Carson booked a motel for them.

As soon as they checked in to their adjoining rooms, Ana said, "Call Jack so I can give him my report while it's fresh. Record the call."

Carson made the call with his cell, on speaker.

She relayed in detail exactly everything Ian had watched her do in the prison cell, describing the space along with the addition of her insights into the inmates. "We're definitely dealing with paranormals. The inmate that was caught is human, the other is a shifter."

"Charles Meduse is a shifter?"

"Yes, and he's not alone. I sensed another presence in the cell and along the escape route. I couldn't see her, but she was there."

"Meduse was reported to have been talking to someone unseen. The guards thought he was developing delusions, some of the other inmates thought he was haunted." Carson said.

"She isn't a dead soul. I'm not sure what she is. I had the sense she was guiding him out. The other inmate was incidental."

"This might explain some of the images on the security footage," Carson said. "Blurred space and a faint impression of a woman's face. The warden thought it was some kind of technical distortion."

"Send it to me when you can," Jack said.

Ian reached for the file folder, leafing through the additional sheets.

Lirikai said, "There were a lot of scents to sort from along the escape path to the riverbank. The prisoners and the guards converged in the same area and sometimes it is difficult to tell them apart. The captured human is dangerous. The shifter inmate smells of greed and self-preservation. He is dangerous if he's threatened. The third presence Ana has mentioned was very hard to lock onto. Too faint."

"The third presence is driving the escape, she's the one that organized the breakout. I couldn't get a solid reading on her either. She's like a ghost, but she's living. She was focused on the river and heading north."

"The human inmate was captured in the woods, incapacitated by what seems to be a jellyfish sting. The Warden said the dogs couldn't pick up the other inmate's scent anywhere on land with the exception of the escape route from the compound." Carson told Jack.

"Ian? You know this area." Jack said.

"The waterways are interconnected here. If they're aquatic shifters, their salt water versus freshwater dependency might be a factor. The easiest, most direct, escape would be out to the ocean or anywhere along the mainland and island coasts. Otherwise, the river flows from connected lake systems north of here, leading all the way down from the St. Lawrence River, which is essentially an inland highway."

"Okay, we'll review the new material and the topography." Jack said.

Ian returned his attention to the papers as Carson spoke to Jack.

There were several stills pulled from the security cameras, which drew his attention. A narrow waver of energy caught in one shot. He'd seen something like that before.

His chest tightened.

The next still stole his breath. The subtle imprint of the female face in the distortion twisted his gut.

It couldn't be.

"Raya Burns."

FOUR

"WAIT HERE TILL I come for you." Raya leveled her stare on Chuck before heading toward the small wooden shack that was the campground office. Hitching her backpack, she cast a quick glance back to ensure he remained hidden in the bushes and prayed he didn't do anything stupid, like let anyone see his face. He'd be all over the news by now.

Awareness heightened, she opened the brittle screen door.

"Well, hello there, how may I help you?" A round faced woman greeted her, turning away from a decade-old computer screen.

"Small tent lot please. One night. Close to the river if you have it."

"Great time of year for hiking. Which way you headed?" The older woman eyed Raya's pack.

"Thinking of trying some mountain trails. Any recommendations?"

The woman nodded, accepting the cash Raya handed her for the lot rental. "Appalachian is popular. Mind, have your bear spray. Can never be too prepared, young and lovely as you are." She smiled, handing Raya her change.

"No worries, Ma'am, I'm prepared whether a predator is on four feet or two. Thank you." She accepted the receipt and campground map indicating her lot for the day.

"Ensure your campfire is out before you go. Trash goes in the bins. Enjoy your stay with us."

Raya went straight toward her camp lot. As soon as the tent was set up, she made her way around to where Chuck was hidden.

"This is tedious, we should just steal a boat."

"Which draws attention and gets us caught. You can't let anyone see you or you're going straight back to your cozy little bunk with your charming cell mate."

Chuck's lips compressed.

Thought so.

Once back at her tent, Chuck ducked inside. Raya set to making lunch like all the other campers. Pulling food from her pack, she watched families wandering among the sites, visiting summer friends and hauling water gear toward the river. She swallowed a pang of regret, quickly averting her gaze from the smallest of children.

Too late for all that now Raya. You've made your choices.

Loading up the stacked paper plates with food, she went into the tent to share it out equally. Chuck's half of the food was gone in minutes.

"Are we on our own all the way to Montreal?"

"Pretty much."

His shoulders dropped. A moment later, his eyes drifted to her barely touched food. She pushed half of it onto his plate, hoping that if he put himself into a food coma, other base needs wouldn't drift into his head.

"Much better than prison slop." He belched and sighed.

Raya stacked her plate on his and went out to drop the plates in the fire pit. As soon as she heard his snores, she went back in, nudged him to roll over and settled in the confines of the tent to sleep a few hours.

At the dinner hour, she did it all again and slept a few more hours.

As evening descended, she stayed out by the fire, banked it a full hour after dark and returned to the tent.

As soon as the shouts and squeals of families faded, they were replaced by music and raucous laughter drifting from the beach front. She pulled the tent down and stored it in the pack.

"Let's go," she said, waving him toward the woods, making their way toward the smell of a bonfire.

The air filtering through the trees grew heavy with beer and weed-laced smoke. Party goers drifted away in twos and threes or more. Seeing an opening, she grabbed Chuck's pack, and moved toward the bonfire, tossing both packs into the flames. She stood a moment, watching to ensure they caught. There was a flare as the fire engorged itself on the nylon fabric of the pack and tent.

"Hey, sweetheart, where's your people?"

Raya looked up at the sound of the slurred words. "Not far."

"Wanna party?" the young man said holding up a beer. "I bet you like to party... a hot chick like you."

"I sure do, why don't you show me where the action's happening?" He'd forget her sooner than if she'd just shut him down. Men didn't react well to rejection.

His inebriated face cracked with a smile, "Knew it!" He tottered, "This way." He swept an arm, sloshing the beer.

She followed him until they reached the edge of the light cast by the bonfire and ducked into the shadows. She had no idea how long it took him to realize she had ditched him.

She suppressed the small part of her that longed for a life of such free abandonment. Such luxuries of youth were long past. There were more important tasks to be done. Much more important.

Ensuring Chuck's safe escape wasn't one of them-it was merely a necessary step along the way.

IAN STARED AT THE still.

It couldn't be.

It couldn't be her.

It was a desperate trick of his eyes.

He *knew* the curve of that cheek, the tilt of those brows, even as obscured as the image was.

"What's the matter, man? You look like you've seen a ghost." Carson said, leaning in to see what Ian was looking at.

I have.

"Is that a face?"

"Yeah. Yeah, it is."

Ana came around to see the still. "I didn't sense the dead in that particular cell. Their energy is different from a shifter's."

Ian swallowed, glad to know she wasn't among the dead, but a ghost all the same. "Ashray. If she's who I think she is, she's an Ashray."

Carson blew out a breath. "*The* Ashray? *Your* Ashray?"

Ian's head jerked, his eyes still drinking in the obscured features.

His gut was flipping one way and rolling back the other.

That beautiful face broke his heart.

It was undeniable. He still yearned for her, given his reaction at the sight of her face. A face caught in the security footage of a prison break.

What the hell was she doing?

He tried to swallow around the sudden tightness in his throat.

Handing the papers back to Carson, he said, "I need a minute to think."

"Sure man, take your time."

Sliding the patio door open, he stepped out onto the balcony and drew in a long deep breath to get a handle on his emotions and allow space for his brain to kick in and do its thing.

Was this the path that Raya had turned onto when they were still together? When the lies and the sneaking around had begun? Part of him had thought she'd found someone else. The other part thought it was something more. No matter how he confronted her, she wouldn't talk to him.

She had shut him out. He'd watched it happening and let her walk away, unwilling to follow.

Seems now he didn't have much of a choice. He'd have to follow.

Or did he? He was here as a favor to Carson, to help him capture an escaped convict. He could simply tell him key information about the rivers' and lakes' personalities and suggest places to look, then go then back to submerging his head in the bottom of another lake.

The problem was, she might be heading for *his* lake. *His* lake? Well, one of his lakes. Was it coincidence? A sick joke? Had she grown to loathe him so much, she'd go for his territory with a convicted human trafficker, knowing how he felt about human filth?

He'd never have pegged her as someone so spiteful.

But people change, as she had been changing.

Maybe this is who she is now.

Flashes of memory hammered through his head.

All their good times, sweet and fun and full of love.

With a shake of his head, the memories tilted and became more orderly images of the decline of their relationship.

Tragedy had struck, setting their relationship off-kilter. She hadn't handled the news of her brother's loss well. It changed her.

The authorities from the beach town in which he had last been known to be living had reported him missing. Given his lifestyle, they presumed overdose or suicide. Clothes and personal belongings were found piled behind a sand dune, his body swallowed by the sea. They had so many other cases to chase. Sorry for the bad news.

Raya had asked him, once, to help her find her brother. Only once. And he'd refused.

The local authorities said he'd gone into the ocean. Inebriated stupidity or willful suicide. Why else would anyone leave their clothes and valuables—wallet, jewelry—on the beach?

He was sure her manipulative mother was pushing her, as she always had, to look for him. Protect him.

Raya never asked Ian again. She turned inward, absorbed by her grief. Denial. She pushed him away. She'd be gone long periods—weeks at time—with no word on where she was going, coming back looking rough. Like she'd been out partying all night, stinking of clubs and back alleys. They began arguing. Then, she just left him. Disappeared like she never existed.

He'd spent the last few years trying to reclaim the life he'd had before their lives had collided.

Ian ran both hands through his hair, then scrubbed them over his face.

I should never have let her slip away.

He'd come to that conclusion in his reclusion.

He had returned to the world to find this, and he could have prevented it.

Despite how much half of his brain said, '*Yes, that's her! How can you not know her?*' the other half said, '*It's someone else. She would never get herself involved in something like this.*'

No, I should have been more understanding. Less self-ish.

This was *his* responsibility.

The Ashray.

Maybe...Maybe he could help her now...Get her off this path she'd ended up on.

If it wasn't too late for her.

Was it?

These people she was associating with... they were exactly the kind of people he loathed. The reason for his disdain of humanity.

Did he *want* to get involved with her again?

She left him. If she still wanted him, she'd have come back.

He was here for Carson. To help his old friend do his job.

Keep it simple.

His shoulders eased.

He drew another deep, steadying breath and went back inside to the others.

Carson and Lirikai were talking quietly while Ana was on her phone. He closed the patio door behind him and waited for her to finish speaking. His mind was starting to come down from its initial overload.

Carson approached him, speaking softly so as not to disrupt Ana's conversation. "She's talking to Maeda again."

Ian nodded.

"Are you still good to work this case, or should I find someone else?" His eyes were steady on Ian's face.

"I'm doing this. I'll find her."

"You're sure it is her?"

Ian nodded.

"Okay, then what do we need to know?"

"I haven't seen her since we broke off."

"Well, she's been busy since then," Ana's voice cut in as she slipped her phone into her pocket. "Very busy," Her eyes slid to Carson. "Maeda is going to send us a file we have on her activities over the last few years. He warned us though, there isn't much information. Sorry it took so long, he had me on hold while he was conferencing with his media guy on the case. Now that we know who she is, he's going to put her photo out as a missing person."

Ian blew out a breath, gut twisting. If the GPSA has a file on her, this wasn't good. Not good at all.

"What did Maeda say about her?" Carson asked.

"Mentions. Whispers." She shrugged. "Just that her legend has been popping up here and there, linked to the underworld. Seems she's building a reputation as a mercenary."

"A mercenary?" That didn't fit with the woman he knew. "Are you sure?"

He reminded himself that they were following this individual because she'd just broken a convicted human trafficker out of prison. He scrubbed a hand over his face.

Ana nodded, "That's what Maeda said. We'll know a little more when he sends us the file that we have on her."

Maybe he was wrong after all. Maybe he'd just wanted to see her face in that still-frame distortion. He picked it up from the table. It wasn't like she was the only Ashray on the planet, as rare as they were. Or possibly, this was some other type of shifter....

While the shot was obscure, to his eyes, it was definitely her face.

"Maybe I'm wrong," he muttered.

"I hope so, too," Carson said. "What of her family? Are they Ashrays too?"

Ian shook his head. "Her father died in an accident when she was young. Her mother and brother are human, as far as I know." He went silent a long, long moment. Their humanity had been a point of contention between her and her mother. A bitter one. The gift had skipped a generation.

"You're not sure?" he pressed.

"Her brother went missing while we were still together." He didn't mention that it was part of the death of their relationship. "Her mother blamed her for it. Somehow, she always expected her to use her abilities to protect him. And failing that, to find him. She wasn't able to."

"That's a harsh situation," Lirikai said, her voice soft.

"Harsh woman; bitter and resentful."

Ana's phone buzzed. She checked the message then brought her laptop over to the table and sat down. A moment later, they were crowded around the small screen reviewing the file Maeda had sent. There were a few ob-scure photos similar to the screen capture they had, but nothing definitive. There were similarities in the images.

She was a water spirit. An Ashray. A ghost.

"Unless we catch her in her solid form, we can't get a sol-id ID. All we have are a list of mentions and speculations in this file. Impressive rumours about her abilities, though." Ana said.

Ian stood back. "She's hard to track. As an Ashray, she doesn't leave behind a scent, like other shifters."

Ana nodded, "Her energy signature is distinct."

"Her scent is detectable while in human form during the day. That's when she's vulnerable. She can only shift at night."

"Okay, let's review all the files again and figure out the best approach."

Ian nodded, "At this point, I think the inmate's scent might be easier to track if he is, in fact, a shifter as well."

"Which I can do without much problem." Lirikai said.

Ian glanced up at her.

"It is what I do. I track criminals by the scent of their...intentions. In the old days, we would track such individuals and deliver the goddess's justice at the bottom of the sea. Protect the innocent from the wicked."

"Now we have legal systems for that." Carson said to his lover, with a quirk of his lips. He turned his attention back to Ian. "We just need to know what we're up against. I'll get the maps so we can study our options."

Ana nodded "I'll print this new file too. If we can follow the timeline of where she's been seen, maybe we can figure out where she's heading now. I'd still keep our attention focused north. That's the impression I picked up at the prison."

Ian really didn't think he was wrong. While part of him desperately prayed he was, the other part of him hoped he wasn't.

The part of him that longed to see her again.

FIVE

"WE SHOULD HAVE STOPPED hours ago."

Chuck's voice hit Raya's last nerve, right in the back of her skull.

"Enough." She rounded on him with enough vehemence to force him back several steps. All night she'd had to remind herself why she was in the middle of the wilderness with this asshole, deflecting questions, complaints, and persistent propositions. She shuddered. Never in a million.

In the last hour, the harder they pressed on, the more aggressive he became.

He grabbed her wrist. "You're going to make me? What? As far as I can tell, you're here to guide me to my uncle." The more miles they had between the prison guards and themselves, the bolder he became.

"I already told you not to touch me. Release my arm."

His fingers bit deeper into the skin, pressing the bones. "What are you going to do, turn into a puddle? Yeah, it's morning, I know you can't shift," he sneered, pulling her closer.

"Yes, the deal is to deliver you to your uncle," she said through clenched teeth.

He grinned, "He must be paying you very well, to go through all this. I can take what I want and dump you here and get back on my own."

"Maybe," she said, jerking her wrist to dislodge his grip. He held fast. "He also wants something you have. Without it, he said, you shouldn't show your face."

Chuck blanched, then swallowed. "So?" he said, his voice losing some of its bravado.

"So, sounds to me like you're not exactly in his good graces, are you now?"

"You still haven't told me why I need you."

She shrugged, waving a hand toward the tree lined river. "Before I began your instructions on how to break you out of your prison, I listened. I listened in very carefully. You talk too much, you know."

"What do you mean?"

"You don't know when to keep your mouth shut. Bragging to your cellmate, the other inmates about who you were, how important you are, who your uncle is. The properties, the cars and boats. Not all at once, of course. In your everyday blathering, it was easy to learn an awful lot about you."

He glanced down as she pressed the blade tip of a large hunting knife he hadn't seen before to the soft flesh next to his Adams' apple. His fingers released her wrist, stepping back, the razor edge left a tiny incision. His hand went his throat, coming away with fresh blood smeared across his fingertips. "You B-"

"Ah-ah," the point immediately rose to his eye level. "Don't finish that thought." She stepped forward. "It wouldn't take me long to find out what you have, that he wants. It's what I do. You, however, don't know the location of where we're supposed to meet."

"You said we were meeting him in Montreal."

"Did I?"

He frowned.

She could see the doubt in his face.

"No one would know to link me to you. You need to stay hidden, as I said many times. I can simply walk away; you're welcome to fend for yourself."

The desire to ditch her was evident on his tired face. She was just as tired as he was. Both at their limit. She'd pushed on longer than usual the night before, in order to put as much distance as possible between the prison and themselves. Humans wouldn't be expected to have come as far.

The whine of a motor in the distance broke the face-off, forcing both of them to step into the cover of the bushes and trees.

While Chuck was watching the boat pass, she slipped away in the dense brush and made her way to her cache site. After several moments, she heard his raised voice call for her, followed by a string of curses.

Ignoring it, she stuck to her plan and made her way to the target campground. She'd let him stew for a little while before collecting him.

Prick.

She could do with five minutes of peace anyway.

This campground office was much like the last one, with the exception of a small television mounted on the wall rolling the local news. The old man behind the counter aimed his remote at the screen, silencing the audio as he shuffled in her direction with a friendly greeting.

Her interaction with him was much the same as with the woman at the last campground, with the exception of the hair rising on the back of her neck. He studied her face with far too keen an eye.

"Just one tent?"

"Yes, sir."

"Where you headed?"

"Appalachian trails."

"Quite a distance from here."

"So I hear," she said, "Any advice?"

He squinted, and after a moment he shrugged, "Just be mindful of predators and hunters, never know when one will pop up."

She nodded and thanked him, then headed for her lot to set up their camp.

When she went back for Chuck, she found only his pile of clothing in the shade of an outcropping of rock and pine trees.

"Shit."

Had he gone, or was he just cooling off from the intense summer heat?

She waited, scanning the constant flow of the Hudson for the purple-blue iridescent bubble of air that supported him in the water. It was difficult to see under the sun's glare. She thought she spotted him floating among the rocks. "Chuck, let's go," she shouted, and turned to step back into the woods.

A sharp sting struck her cheek followed by flare of pain. "Mother fucker!" she spun back toward the river, pulling her knife.

A clear, thin cord shot toward her from the water, wrapping around her wrist. She grunted from the pain of the poison burning the sensitive skin, "Come out, you son of a bitch!" she snarled as her blade slashed at the cord, releasing her arm, and she backed further away from the river. Another tentacle shot toward her, falling short, and retracted back into the water. She sheathed the knife.

"Fuck. Fuck!" Her fingers wiped the blood dribbling along her cheekbone, the fire of his poison mingling with it, seeping into her blood stream faster than the wound on her wrist. She sheathed her knife, stumbling back through the woods, running for the campground. The last image she saw was the enormous smudge of a bright yellow and pink inflatable ducky before she fell to the dirt path, unconscious.

IAN AND THE TEAM made their way to a small community hospital not far from their motel.

The call had come in not an hour past that someone matching Raya's description had been seen and taken by ambulance from a campground further up the Hudson than they'd expected.

Releasing her photograph to the local networks as a missing person had worked, and they'd received calls from the campgrounds she'd been to, as well as some campers that had seen her. However, they hadn't anticipated a trip to the hospital. A family had called the ambulance when she collapsed on the path in front of them, on their way to the campground beach.

Ian told administration he was her partner-the one looking for her. The story they concocted was that she suffered from depression, stopped her meds and took off. He told them how relieved he was to have found her again, safe.

The hospital staff weren't sure what was wrong with her. They surmised it may be a severe allergic reaction to some kind of poison parsnip or oak or ivy, maybe. They were keeping her stable and comfortable.

The team hung back in the hospital corridor while Ian stood in the open doorway staring at the bed, heart hammering.

"Do you want us to stay here?"

"No. I'd like a few moments."

"We'll look for the cafeteria, then come back in a bit."

Carson's hand squeezed Ian's shoulder before he took Lirikai's hand and followed Ana down the hall.

Ian's feet were rooted.

For the first time in his life, he was frozen in place while his insides churned.

She'd left him, after weeks of relationship disintegration. Half-truths and lies, avoidance and periodic disappearances.

He'd confronted her, and she'd dissolved what they were in that very moment.

When she walked out, she left him in a state of confusion, distrust, shock, and heartbreak.

All of that warred within him now. Surging. Renewed. Fresh.

He still loved her.

She was his heart.

He'd known it when they'd met all those years ago.

He just thought she knew it too.

It seemed she had, at least for a while.

He drew a deep breath, swallowed down the renewed hurt, resentment and confusion and stepped toward the bed.

She lay so still.

Pale.

Her face was relaxed in induced sleep. A bandage taped to her cheekbone was a stark white slash against the rich sunlit bronze of her skin. He reached for her hand, staring at the bandages encircling her delicate wrist.

"Ray." His whisper was loud in the silence of the room as he brought her fingers to his lips.

Sedated as she was, he didn't expect a response.

Her hair was a thick cloud of dark curls around her head, her lashes were silky fans, her brows delicate jet arches. His gaze dropped to her wide, full mouth, wanting to see her brilliant smile again.

His right hand held hers, thumb stroking her fingers while his other scrubbed over his face with a deep sigh.

This was so fucked up.

She was here, in this bed, because she'd broken an inmate out of prison and gone on the run.

Why?

Not to mention the GPSA file hinting at her exploits over the last years-the years since she'd walked out on him.

His jaw clenched as he stared at the beautiful face he loved, trying to reconcile the two realities of who he knew her to be with what she had become.

He wasn't sure he could.

His fingers brushed the tape holding the bandage on her wrist. Carefully, he eased back the edges hoping to not find what he suspected was there.

It was. Several rows of whip-like purple welts burned into the flesh identical to those found on the second escapee encircled her wrist.

"Bollocks." There was no denying her connection to the same inmate.

So what happened? Whatever it was, he was going to find out what was going on.

He'd come onto the case as a favor to Carson. A consultant. Now, he was going to see this through to wherever it took them.

Gently placing her hand back on the blanket next to her, his fingers lingered over hers for another moment before he left to search for Carson. It would be a little while longer before the sedation lifted.

SIX

THE DISTINCT SCENT OF hospital disinfectant crowded Raya's senses first. Then the sounds of voices and the sense of movement in the distance.

Raya's eyes fluttered open, and squeezed shut against the glare of sunlight piercing her eyes. Her head throbbed, her face and wrist ached.

She clenched her fists against the heart pounding need to leave the building.

This wasn't good. She hated hospitals. Really hated them.

And she was hallucinating.

Amid the sun glare was a hazy image of what she could have sworn was Ian.

Tongue plastered to the inside of her mouth, she tilted her head away from the window. Several figures were in various states of lounging, between her bed and the door.

She blinked, trying to focus on the unfamiliar faces. "Who are you?" she croaked.

A tall, dark-haired man stepped toward, while one of the women with him discretely closed the door. "Carson Perenga. GPSA."

"Shit," she groaned. Not just a hospital. Busted by law enforcement. She'd failed. And failed bad.

"Ray." The deep, distinct voice drew her attention back toward the widow. Her breath lodged in her chest.

"Am I doped up, or is that you, Ian?"

"It's me."

So bad.

Turning her face away from both men, she instead stared at the ceiling, hoping to find sense in the tiny holes of the tiles. Surely, she was locked in a nightmare.

Her nails bit into her palms as her fists clenched tighter.

"Why the hell are you here?" Her voice was hoarse, harsh, even. She squeezed her eyes shut to stop the sudden surge of tears from escaping as her heart flipped and rent. After years of suppressing her emotions and maintaining a controlled state, those two words had just ripped open all the pain and memories she'd shut away—locked away for good, she had thought.

She'd never expected to hear that voice again. Should never have hoped for it.

Especially in these circumstances. Her heart ached and she swallowed hard. She couldn't look at him. She couldn't face the judgment in his eyes. She didn't want to relive the pain of the circumstances around their breakup.

Because she couldn't tell him the truth. He wouldn't understand.

She considered her options.

She was caught. These were feds.

Would they arrest her?

Or help her?

Why the hell was Ian here?

The lake. Of course. She had considered the possibility he might be there before she initiated the project. Her last report had him in the west at Okanagan. She'd just hoped he would stay far away.

She needed to get out of here. She had a job to finish. There was too much at stake and this was no time for wallowing in the heartache of betrayal.

She reeled it all back into the safety of her anger.

"Why are you here?" she said again, through clenched teeth. Her head still throbbed; her body ached.

He stood and approached her bed.

She turned her head and leveled her stare on his face, coming into focus. Her brain promptly went to war with her heart and her hormones.

She'd nearly forgotten how handsome he was. That was a lie—she'd tried to forget. And she couldn't ignore the fact that despite the circumstances, every part of her reacted to him like the gravity between the moon and the tide. Her fingers twitched toward him. She flexed her fingers out in an effort to dispel the stiffness, but they just resumed their curled state as she waited for him to speak.

His broad shoulders shielded her from the sun and it took a moment for her eyes to focus on his face in shadow as he moved in and out of the light.

Still strong and serious. His brows were drawn down, and his eyes held a deep weariness as he regarded her. His normally full mouth was tight. She realized she wanted to ease the lines and see him smile again, just for a moment or two. With a blink, she discarded that thought.

"I'm here for you." He said.

Her heart foolishly jumped.

No, he was here with the GPSA.

"Well, here I am."

"Where is Charles Meduse?" Agent Perenga asked, breaking the spell that was threatening to draw her too far into the current of Ian's aura.

"Who?"

Ian picked up her wrist. "Your inmate lover."

She tried to snatch it away, but he held fast as she choked on the word. "Lover?"

He didn't really believe that. Did he? She looked into his eyes. No. He was pushing.

She pushed back. "I have many lovers, can you be more specific?"

His frown deepened and his lips thinned even more.

Good.

One of the women stepped forward. To Agent Perenga she said, "This is a waste of time, I can track him."

Perenga seemed to consider this as he turned back to Raya. "Who is Meduse meeting? Who hired you to break him out?"

Chuck was just a lead.

Looks like they're after the same thing I am.

Maybe.

"Again. Who?"

The other woman remained by the wall. "She isn't going to talk. There's too much at stake."

"If she won't cooperate, we'll have to arrest and detain her."

"On what charge? Camping?"

"On suspicion of aiding and abetting a fugitive felon from a prison."

"There is no proof of such a ridiculous claim."

"Isn't there?" Perenga said, voice even.

Raya let her silence speak for her.

"You'll have to move her during the day and hold her in a place with no flowing water source. No pipes or underground streams." Ian said.

Her face whipped his direction.

Traitor.

Perenga nodded. He turned to the woman next to him. "Lirikai, track him, but don't engage. I want to see who he meets with. That's more important right now. We can retrieve him later."

She nodded, brushed a delicate hand down his arm and went out of the room.

"Ortega, stay here with Ian. Get what you can."

"She's hard to read." Ortega said, voice so low Raya almost missed it. "The emotional confusion is blocking everything else out right now."

Perenga nodded. "Keep trying." To Ian he said, "I'm going to secure a holding facility."

As soon as he left, Raya studied the small woman left behind. "What are you, a fortune teller?" She taunted with a smirk.

Agent Ortega straightened her slight shoulders, not rising to the bait.

"How long have you been a mercenary?" Ian's voice stung her.

Her heart flipped. Raya clamped her emotions in place with a steel trap and remained silent.

"Working for money. I thought you were a peace-loving naturalist. Money had little value. At least, that's how I remember you, until just before the end."

"Do you remember? Truly?" She shot back. "Do you remember how you betrayed me?"

"Betrayed you?" Ian's voice rose. "You spent weeks lying and deceiving me before you left me."

"I left you because you betrayed me. The lies were necessary."

"Like fuck." He leaned toward her. "Since when is it necessary to lie to someone you're supposed to love?"

"When he refused to support you."

Ian stepped back. "When didn't I support you?" His voice softened, floating over her, confusion evident on his face.

"The only time in all the years we spent together that I asked you to help me. The only time. If you couldn't do that one thing, then we couldn't *be*."

The color drained from his face.

She swallowed the heartache lodged in her throat.

"Why didn't you help me, Ian?" Her words steamrolled toward him. "Couldn't be bothered to leave your precious lake and go out into the wider world? Too much trouble to disrupt your peaceful existence to look for Dominique?" She could see the truth of her words strike him.

"They said he was dead."

"*Probably* dead."

"Your mother had no right to drop responsibility for his life on your shoulders."

"It was *my* choice."

"There was evidence, Raya. His clothes, identification, his ring-"

"There was no body."

"The sea took him, Raya."

"That's what they told us. I've learned, that's what they tell everyone."

He straightened his shoulders, as he did when he was uncomfortable.

"Raya, I..." He blew out a breath, turning to the window.

She ignored the slip of emotion in his voice, the flash of conflicting pride and...regret?

"I thought you loved me enough to help me with this one thing I needed help with. *He* had nothing to do with what happened to your family all those years ago. I mistakenly believed *I* might have been more important than your grudges and prejudices. I was wrong."

The silence was a barrier that widened with every passing second.

"You are." He turned back from the window, expression set.

Anger surged through her. "Clearly I'm wrong, you don't need to-"

"You are more important." His words froze the breath in her chest.

Her heart expanded and retracted as she studied him. The regret was raw.

"It's too late."

SEVEN

IAN REPLAYED THE MEMORY of her expression when he told her she was more important.

The words were out of his mouth before the thoughts had entered his head. It was like some other part of him had overridden his battered pride and deeply buried shame.

A fissure of shocked disbelief cracked the anger etched into Raya's lovely face. She slammed it closed. Those words meant something to her.

She refused to say anything more after that.

The hospital discharged her to his care and they were on route to the interim holding facility. Ian had recalled that a mutual friend of his and Carson's had a cabin up in the mountains, suggesting it as a possible option. He hadn't been there since before their friend had built on the land, so had no idea what the place was like.

Carson called Odson, and they were in luck. The cabin was available and lacked running water. There was a rain-water holding tank, otherwise they would need supplies.

Carson drove while Ana used her phone to find a nearby village where they could get supplies.

Ian's gaze was pulled back to Raya's profile.

She hadn't spoken to him again. Her attention was fixed on the rolling landscape outside her window, or straight ahead through the windshield.

"There's a small convenience store in the next town. If you turn off this main road, we should find a grocery store." Ana said to Carson.

As the car slowed to make the turn at the intersection, Raya's door snapped open at the same time she released her seatbelt and jumped out.

"Raya!" Ian yelled as he struggled to release his own seatbelt. "Stop, Carson."

Getting out of the SUV he took off after her across the road, nearly getting himself hit by oncoming traffic.

She disappeared into the dense brush lining the road and he barreled in after her. He had the advantage of long legs to keep up to her gazelle-like pace as she nimbly dodged overhanging branches and ground debris.

"Raya, stop!"

She didn't.

He was nearly upon her, despite the extra effort his larger body exerted to avoid the same obstacles she had.

"Don't make things harder for yourself. Give it up."

His hand stretched for the back of her shirt.

She spurred forward. His fingers closed on air.

Raya dodged around a cluster of trees and changed direction, putting extra distance between them, running along a rock ledge.

Goddess, she was fast.

He remembered the days spent hiking and running together. This was different. It was like she trained for this kind of scenario.

It was daylight, so he knew she couldn't shift. She was likely trying to lose him in the forest until she could find a place to hide from him and the agents.

His legs pumped hard and he leapt, reaching.

Making contact, they rolled hard over the uneven forest floor, grunting as hard branches and rocks hit limbs and ribs.

They came to a stop with him atop her. She fought as he struggled to grab her wrists to pin her to the ground.

"Give up," he growled as his beast-self rose to the surface after the chase and capture.

"I'll never give up." She snarled back.

She somehow managed to fold herself so that her knees and feet came up between them, and sent him flying away from her. She instantly scrambled to her feet, hands clenched into fists.

"Don't be so stubborn." He said, gasping for breath after having the force of her feet lodged in his gut.

"*I'm* stubborn? Look who's talking, you goddamned hypocrite. You're the one that is stubbornly holding on to centuries' old grudges and outdated ways of thinking."

"That has nothing to do with what's happening right now. You can't expect to not face the consequences of breaking a human trafficker out of prison, Raya. When did you lose your mind?"

Her eyes narrowed on him. The rosy hue of her cheeks darkened several shades more before she came at him.

She was a churning whirlpool of fists and feet, striking him like dead wood in a frothing river rapids.

He hadn't expected her to attack him. He'd been as naive as a careless young lad entering his first battle, guard down. He deserved it when her shoe flashed before his eyes, causing the world to go black.

STUBBORN? GIVE UP?

Not. Fucking. Likely.

The suppressed rage of a lifetime of being dictated to rose up in the form of her fists.

The loss of her father at a young age. The manipulation and resentment of her mother ever since. The self-harm and loss of her only brother.

Ian's failure to support her when she needed him most. She hadn't realized how deep and raw the erosion of those last years were until faced with the reality of his proximity now.

He still expected her to walk away—because he wanted her to.

This was more important than his precious pride, or her wounded heart.

This was her brother's life.

This was the lives of many others besides.

She had to get Chuck to Montreal so she could fulfill the next part of what she'd set out to do so many years before. And she couldn't do that from a GPSA prison.

This was the first time in years that she found herself hesitating to act.

They were giving her no choice.

He was giving her no choice.

He was another obstacle to overcome.

She let her rage power the strikes of her fists and feet to drown out the knowledge that she was striking Ian.

Ian.

The fissure in the dam had crumbled the barrier and the torrent was wild. She used the emotional super charge to find her equilibrium again.

She was too close to let them stop her now. She couldn't fail.

She sprang forward, taking advantage of his shock.

Every impact struck her heart, below the rage. The shock on his face seared her soul. She already regretted it, but couldn't let it hinder the need to escape. She had to try.

She'd learned how to drop a man much bigger than herself since the last time she'd seen Ian.

And she did.

A fraction of a second later, she drew a weary breath and turned to run, only to be met with the furious face of Agent Ortega, arm extended in her direction with a device in her hand, her chest heaving from the pursuit.

Raya's eyes swept the device. It was a Taser. Agent Perenga crashed through the woods toward them, still at a distance.

She raised her fists. "You'll go down faster than he did. Just let me go."

"No." Ortega's eyes were locked on Raya. "You owe me a new pair of shoes, Burns."

"Maybe if I can finish this job, I'll be able to afford it. Last time. Walk away."

Ortega adjusted her aim.

Raya hoped Ortega was more desk than field agent, and a poor shot, as she gauged the distance.

Was she faster than Ortega's trigger finger?

She had to try.

Raya turned in an attempt to outrun the reach of the Taser probes.

Ortega didn't have a slow trigger finger, nor was she a poor shot, Raya conceded as the probes struck her back, causing her to crumple to the ground not far from Ian's inert body.

She was so fucked.

EIGHT

IAN RODE IN THE backseat next to Raya, her wrist cuffed to his to prevent her from running again. Ana rode up front with Carson, and Lirikai hadn't checked in yet.

Ian's face and abdomen ached; his pride was shredded.

Raya maintained her silence during the long drive north and up into the mountains. The landscape here was veined with rivers and creeks feeding into the Hudson. They stopped only once for supplies. They had to get to wherever they were going before dark.

Ian couldn't stop himself from glancing in Raya's direction. With her attention trained on the passing landscape, it was easier for him to drink in what he could see of her face. No matter that she looked the same, she felt different to him. She even smelled a little different. The sweet innocence of her scent was altered.

Proved when her fist had connected with his face.

He should be furious that she'd struck him. He was still in disbelief.

She definitely was not the sweet Raya Burns he'd known. *That* woman would never commit violence on another individual.

This was *his* fault.

He swallowed his guilt.

He should have helped her look for her brother. Instead, Ian just accepted that he'd died of a drug overdose or committed suicide while vacationing on the coast. That's what the local police told them when they handed her Dominique's belongings, that's what Ian went with.

Not Raya.

She wanted more proof. They both knew the hunger of the sea and how unlikely the probability that she would give up a body.

Raya's mother expected the impossible of her.

"How is your mother?"

She started at the sound of his voice. "Dead."

"I'm sorry." Despite being human, she was still Raya's mother, and a compatriot.

Raya sighed, and nodded at his acknowledgment. "I know you didn't care for her. Her liver finally gave out." After another long moment, she added, "I brought her remains home to Aberdeen and buried my father's ashes with her. Resting together where they started, back in Scotland. Before life turned to shit for them." She sighed. "Now it's just me."

Alone.

Instinct prompted Ian to slip his fingers around hers on the seat between them.

She looked down at their hands. A break in the trees allowed the sun to catch on the cuffs linking their wrists. Her hand slid out from under his, fingers curling against her thigh.

The loss of her touch was razor-sharp.

Carson turned the car onto a dirt road—if you could call it that. It reminded Ian more of the old narrow tracks criss-crossing the countryside before automobiles were a thought. He appreciated the modern suspension as they bounced along under the thick canopy of trees for an eternity before coming to a stop in front of a shack.

"Lovely," Raya muttered.

Ana's sigh echoed the sentiment.

"Just like the old days, eh, Ian?" Carson quipped.

Stacked log walls sagged over a stone foundation, topped with a crumbling, lichen-covered roof. "Looks like Odson built this place himself." Ian eyed the place.

Carson shrugged. "You seen him lately?" He asked as he parked the car and popped the trunk.

"It's been a couple of decades, but aye." He grabbed two of the large water jugs from next to Raya's backpack in the trunk. With Raya in tow, still attached by the cuffs, Ian headed toward the cabin.

Inside the cabin it was easier to see its fortress-like qualities. The interior structure was bolstered. Every corner was precise and immaculate. The support columns were intricately carved in the old style with mythical beasts and flora. Drawn to them, he stared a long time.

"Ian?" Ana's voice broke the reverie that was blocking out the present.

"Yeah?" He smiled, shoving the sudden nostalgia down where it belonged. Buried.

Ana handed him more supplies and turned back to the car.

"Are you going to uncuff me at some point? Being tugged back and forth is getting tedious." Raya said.

"Are you going to start talking about Charles Meduse and your camping trip?" Ian asked.

"May as well get comfortable. Until we can figure out which GPSA facility can house you best, you're stuck here with them." Carson nodded toward Ana and Ian as he went back outside.

"Wait, what? Why do I have to stay here? There's no working toilet, Carson." Ana's voice drifted off as she followed him.

Ian gave Carson a full description of the topography of the lake region and the waters' personalities to relay to Lirikai. He told Carson he should be doing the scouting, since that's what he had called him in to do. Carson insisted it was more important he stay with Analiese and Raya.

"Maybe you can find the right words to get her to work with us." He finally said.

By the time Carson abandoned them to the quiet of the mountain forest, they had enough supplies to last quite a few days.

Ana paced back and forth outside, hand extended to the heavens, trying to catch a signal on her cell. She didn't believe him when he told her there likely weren't any cell towers out here yet—if there ever would be.

She went back inside a quarter hour later, cursing and muttering under her breath.

"Come on, we may as well make dinner," he suggested, looking through the cupboards at the dishes. "Raya, do you remember how to make scones?"

They found the cabin to be powered by a solar powered generator. Cords of wood were piled around back for the wood stove, in the event the generator failed and they needed to cook.

She gave him a level look and rolled her eyes. Ignoring it, he grinned. "Ana, Ray and I will teach you how to make the best scones on the planet."

"I don't think you should let her near the cutlery. I've read her files."

"Really, now?" He turned toward Raya with a raised brow. "Well. This ought to be interesting; may as well regale us with these mercenary tales. Good with fists, feet *and* weapons?"

She had been desperate to escape earlier that day. How far would she go to gain that freedom?

Raya turned her impassive face toward Ana. "Knives or spatulas," She shrugged. "I can make either equally effective."

Ian shoved a plastic bowl in Raya's hands followed by a whisk. "Come on now, Ray, don't try to frighten the lass." He intentionally thickened his burr, drawing her attention, and smiled. Since she'd grown up in eastern North America, she'd always said how much she liked the sound of his accent when he wasn't masking it.

Her frown dropped back into place.

It was worth a try.

Carson preferred her cooperation to incarceration. Ian agreed.

At one time, he would have said he knew Raya better than anyone. Did he still? Even though she'd changed so much?

He slid measured ingredients across the counter and, having nothing else to do, she began mixing while Ian chatted with Ana. Raya remained silent beside him. She was slowly losing the brittle tension that stiffened her body.

He didn't know if he could get her to tell them what they needed to know. Given the reputation she seemed to have earned, he'd have to give her a damned good reason to say anything. A damned good reason.

Aside from keeping her confined, that's what they were here to do.

NINE

RAYA'S EYES WERE GLUED to Ian's regrettably bruised face as they sat at the tiny table eating the scones and drinking tea in near silence.

The sudden roll of Ian's brogue earlier had jolted her back a decade. He knew that the wicked combination of that brogue and his boyish smile used to drop her panties faster than anything else in the world. And the scones.

He was working her.

She couldn't let him see it wasn't taking much effort to have an impact on her.

No matter how this was bringing back memories; memories of him making her scones for breakfast in nothing but an apron. The view from behind was a wonderful distraction while she waited.

She blinked away the traitorous memory as the buttery food slid over her tongue.

She was so focused on Ian, she was nearly startled to recall Ortega was there watching her, small and timid looking. Raya clearly saw Ortega's catlike patience as she surveyed her.

Raya had had plenty of opportunity to build her poker-face over the years.

But this, with Ian, had never been a factor.

She was going to have to make some decisions.

Her job was to get Chuck safely to his Uncle via Montreal, with a slight detour to retrieve something he valued. Raya suspected the item was the real goal in all this and the nephew was actually just a bonus of sorts.

Why wasn't her employer telling her what it was? A flare for the dramatic? Was it so she wouldn't have time to over think and change course if it was something of monetary value? Clearly, he didn't yet trust her enough. A test of some sort, no doubt.

Either way, she needed to complete the job. She needed to get close to this man. He was the key.

Her eyes slid to Ian again. Why was he here? What did he have to gain from this? He never mentioned working for the Global Paranormal Security Agency before. He was a recluse. Part of GPSA's job was to protect humans from rogue paranormals, which was entirely out of his character.

She recalled the banter between him and Carson. A favor for a long-time friend, no doubt.

He couldn't do her a 'favor' to help her find her brother.

The scone turned gritty in her mouth and she placed the remainder back on her plate. Their cuffed hands rested side by side on the scarred wooden tabletop.

They were going to send her to a GPSA prison. Her throat was too tight to swallow. If she went to prison now, she'd never be able to find Dominique. She had to find out if he was still alive or truly dead.

She looked up to see agent Ortega assessing her.

"What do you want from me?" she asked, even though she already knew.

"We want to know who Chuck Meduse is going to meet. When and where."

"What do you plan to do with me?"

Ortega sighed, considering her. "Depends."

Raya raised a brow, waiting for her to elaborate.

Ortega thought a long moment before answering. "Obviously, breaking an inmate out of jail is illegal. However, you know we couldn't prosecute you through the human judicial system, you'd have to go through GPSA's system. As Charles Meduse *should* have done." She leaned back, re-crossing her legs on the chair and shrugged. "Reduced time. Depends how good your intel is."

Reduced time.

That wasn't enough. Raya seriously considered her options. "Has my detention been made public?"

"Not yet. The only reports were those of an unknown female taken from a camping ground to hospital to be treated for exhaustion and dehydration."

"Who in your department knows I've been caught?"

"Our team and director."

"Keep it that way, and I'll help you retrieve Chuck, for full immunity."

Ortega's eyes narrowed. "Full immunity. That's a big ask. We'd need more—a lot more. Besides, how could we be assured you can be trusted?"

Raya turned her attention to Ian, who was observing in silence, his keen eyes on her face. She looked at the cuffs for a long moment before she turned her focus back to Ortega. "We're after the same thing. You want Chuck's boss, right? Chuck's Boss is his uncle. Maybe you know that already. What you may not know is that he wants Chuck to retrieve something of value before going to meet him. Which I was supposed to ensure that he did. That's what he's paying me to do."

She looked at Ian. "I'll let you have him after I get what I need from him. I need information about the trafficking network."

Ian blinked, lips compressing.

"That's what we're after." Ortega said.

"I need the intelligence for the organization I'm *actually* working for. An organization that exists solely to infiltrate and break this network."

"Why not just work with GPSA? I highly doubt they aren't aware of this organization you mentioned?"

"This is bigger than your serve and protect organization."

"So, you're working as a mercenary to infiltrate this crime organization." Ian said, his disbelief weighing his voice. "Is this for real?"

She nodded.

"You really have changed."

"You haven't."

He jerked from the sting of her words.

"I'll need to report to Agent Perenga and our director." Ortega said.

"If you wait too long, it'll be too late."

"We have no choice until he comes back."

HOW HAD SHE GONE from wanting to find her brother to this?

Ian's stomach rolled and tightened.

If the two weren't connected, how had she landed on this incredulous path? As a mercenary. Working for some shadow organization.

All this time?

He scrubbed a hand over his face trying to process what she'd said as he looked at her, trying to find the truth in her words, in their current situation.

It seemed everything had changed between them in a snap of her fingers. So many times, he'd thought of the night she asked for his help.

He regretted the devastation on her face when she'd asked him to help find her brother and he shut her down.

That should never have happened.

He'd been a stubborn, selfish, arsehole.

It shouldn't have mattered that he believed her damned mother guilt-twisted her into going, just as with everything else she wanted Raya to do.

Raya and her brother spent their lives firmly under their mother's thumb, to the point where he had fallen into addiction, no matter how much Ray had tried to help him.

To Ian, it hadn't been a surprise when they were told he was missing and presumed to have committed suicide or overdosed at the beach where he was living.

Her mother had instilled this impossible sense of responsibility for the kid, no matter that he was a full-grown man that had maintained a youthful appearance, with red hair and freckles that stood out on pale skin, like their mother's. Ray favored her father's rich brown skin and thick curly hair—he'd often caught her staring at the one family photo she had.

Ian really believed the kid was lost and he'd just wanted Raya to have some peace. Devoid of her mother's demands and the responsibility of looking out for her kid brother all the time. And selfishly, he'd wanted her to live in peace with him, away from the chaotic world of humans.

He never dreamed she would go down this path.

She was an Ashray, with an inherent need to seek sanctuary and live in places of beauty.

Yet here she was, living the life of an undercover mercenary, hip deep in the lowest of human filth.

No. This wasn't the human underbelly. This prisoner was a paranormal working within the network. How many others were there? He'd come to think of humans as primitive little savages after they destroyed the relationship of peaceful co-existence between themselves and his family. But paranormals using their strengths to enslave the weak wasn't acceptable either.

He looked up into Raya's defiant face, staring him down.

She'd become someone else.

Her accusation that he hadn't changed stung.

Why? Why would he be stung by that? He'd been around for centuries, what did it matter if he changed or not?

Somehow the fact that she believed he hadn't, mattered to him.

He wasn't sure he liked how much she had changed.

Had she changed so much in the ways that truly mattered?

This wasn't about chasing a life of darkness for gain. It was about finding information for a covert organization to combat global human trafficking.

What the hell?

What if that was just a lie? A lie to convince them to let her go on her merry way?

He'd believed her lies before. Lies to hide her activities because she knew he'd try to stop her from looking for her brother.

He should have helped her find closure. Her mother's involvement shouldn't have mattered. Ian should have just supported Raya. Helped her. Maybe none of this would have happened. She wouldn't be facing time in a GPSA prison—if she was lying.

They'd still be together. Not in this ridiculous situation.

She broke an inmate out of a prison. He had to admit, that was a fucking ballsy thing to do.

He'd spent far too much time moping in his lakes.

Ian couldn't be sure one way or the other of the truth. He glanced at Ortega. If this was all a lie, Raya was facing serious prison time. Could he live with himself knowing she was shut away in a cell?

If she was telling the truth, then she was working in a fucking dangerous climate, and only looking to sink deeper.

Where would it end? Would she drown, and her bones be swallowed by the ocean, too? Or could she surface triumphant and be free, once and for all?

He held Raya's gaze. "Maybe it's serendipitous that Carson called me, and that I actually agreed to help him. Or maybe I just got tired of the boredom of being alone with my own thoughts." He drew a deep breath and blew it out. "Either way, I'm here to help." He slipped his hand around Raya's slender fingers, brushing his thumb over her soft skin. "It's late in the game, I know." He stopped to draw another deep breath. "I'm going to help you, Ray, as I should have done years ago. I failed you."

His heart cracked at the sudden gathering of tears in her eyes. A fissure of deep regret shot through that crack when she blinked them away, straightened her spine and gave him a sharp nod, mask snapped back in place.

TEN

IT'S LATE IN THE game, I know. ... I'm going to help you, Ray, as I should have done years ago. I failed you.

Those words rolled through Raya's mind over and over. *I failed you.*

She'd never known Ian to apologize to anyone in the years they were together.

No one had ever apologized to her. Ever, in her life.

Ian, in his way, had.

Yes, it was late coming.

She couldn't deny how hard those words hit her. Like a throat punch.

She sighed, staring at the far wall of the dark room, laying on her side, the heat from Ian's body radiating against her back.

Still cuffed together, until agent Perenga returned with the keys, they lay in the cabin's one bedroom, while agent Ortega curled up on the couch, the door open between them.

Ignoring the awkward angle of her arm with her right hand resting on the bed behind her, next to Ian's, Raya tried to process the turmoil of her thoughts and emotions. This job was not going the way she'd planned. She and

Chuck should have been reaching their final camp soon, then retrieving his uncle's precious object before going on to the yet to be determined meeting point.

What the hell was she going to do now?

Would the other agents catch Chuck?

From all the hours spying on Chuck before engaging him and instigating the breakout, she'd listened. He talked up the condo he had in Montreal. Where he stored his sports cars and kept expensive art. Where he partied with beautiful women who threw themselves at him. Gag.

What a yammerhead. She was pretty sure the only reason Chuck worked for the Quebec City crime boss Jean-Guy LeVoleur was because he was his sister's son. Otherwise, she had no doubt he'd be cemented under a sidewalk somewhere, because the guy never shut his yap. A *secret* condo that he kept to himself, that he didn't think his uncle knew about.

Well he knew of its existence, just not its precise location. That was part of Raya's job. If she couldn't get Chuck to the condo to get the thing, then it was up to her to retrieve it herself.

Either way, she preferred to deliver Chuck at the meeting. She had a reputation to maintain in order to navigate the underworld. An unavoidable necessity.

She hadn't lost control of a job so badly since the early days when she fumbled her way along. In this line of work, she'd had to learn fast.

Lost in her thoughts, she didn't notice the change in Ian's breathing and was startled when he rolled onto his side. His heavy arm arched over and around her, with her back suddenly pressed against his chest, her backside to his groin. With her right hand wedged in the small of her back, the rim of Ian's navel was distinct against her curled fingers.

Surprised, she remained still, Chuck gone from her head to be filled by the sensation of Ian's body against hers.

He grew hard against her.

She should ease away from him.

The familiar, old desire to rub her ass against him was overwhelming. The invitation for him to slip into her. The memory of how he used to fill her slammed her body, and sent a coil of heat shooting down her belly to pool in her panties. The lightning reaction of her body to his took her breath away.

She ached for him.

His scent enveloped her. She closed her eyes, resisting the urge to breathe deeply of him. His big hand curled next to her chest, just under her chin. Part of her wished it would slip over her breast. Her nipples hardened. It was so difficult not to move her hips against him.

So familiar. His body was like home.

She should move away, regardless of probably waking him.

She didn't.

Instead, she closed her eyes and slowly—very slowly—relaxed her body. The heat of his body seeped into the muscles of her rigid back. The more she allowed herself to ease into him, the tighter his arm pulled her to the comforting realm of his chest.

Her throat tightened.

She had no idea how much she missed this—how much she missed him—until this very moment. The fingers of her free hand curled over his and pressed it to her beating heart. Like it had just suddenly kick-started again after years of being dormant.

It hurt.

She didn't stop the tears when they came this time, allowing the edge of her pillow to absorb them as she finally fell asleep.

"Ian."

His eyes snapped open at the whisper of his name.

Ana stood by the open door of the bedroom. "It's morning."

He nodded and she disappeared.

He took stock of his situation.

Curled into his chest like she was meant to be there, Raya's breathing was steady in sleep. His hand was entwined with hers, pressed to her chest. Her bottom rested against his groin and thighs and all he could smell was her hair and the natural scent of her skin. Fresh like a natural spring after a long winter. He studied the fine hairs curled at her nape, resisting the urge to graze his lips over the soft skin. Her breasts were soft against his forearm and her firm arse brought back a rush of memory that had him hard without another thought.

Sensing his arousal, she leaned back into him and he swallowed a groan, staying as still as possible, for as long as possible. It was delicious torture. He remained as he was. His greedy mind was lost in a feast of delectable flesh amid soft moans of delight, his memories of their passion vivid in the dull morning light. He knew this body so well. He knew what made her breath catch and what made her moan, and especially what made her scream.

He grew harder. Bad idea. He strained against his jeans' zipper, having slept as they were, fully clothed. His body craved hers in a way he hadn't acknowledged before now. There'd been no thought, no interest to find someone else when she left him. Now, with her lithe body pressed to his as she was, there was no doubt in the hunger that was surfacing.

Ana wandered past the open door, folding the blanket she'd used and straightening the pillows on the couch.

He had to focus on that.

No matter how much he craved slipping into Ray, watching the passion in her expression and the little sounds he knew she would make as he loved her—it wasn't going to happen. No matter how much he ached. The need was a vice around his chest.

Her breathing lightened and he knew she was awake. After an eternal moment she leaned away. The cool morning air rushed to fill the new space between them. Sitting up on the edge of the bed, she looked down at him. Her expression not as hard as it was the day before, as she studied him.

"Good morning." He said, voice husky, brogue thick.

She smiled, and he could feel the sun rise in his chest.

ELEVEN

RAYA SERIOUSLY CONSIDERED HER options as she looked around at the cabin in the early morning light.

She was still cuffed to Ian. The key was miles and miles away, secured in agent Perenga's pocket.

She'd never had the opportunity to master handcuff lockpicking, so that was out. As was severing Ian's hand from his wrist. She was dedicated to her job, but maiming him wasn't an option. She wasn't so ruthless that she'd take such drastic measures to free herself from Ian. Were it Chuck, she'd think about it. The other douche-bag, Glenn, she wouldn't think twice.

All this time, she'd been watching and listening to Ian and the GPSA agents—and to her gut—trying to find a bead of light in the shadows of her situation. If she was honest with herself, which she usually was, that bead of light was Ian, of all things and people. She was beginning to believe maybe she could work with these agents.

Maybe.

The cabin's three occupants tried to find things to fill their time throughout the long day.

Ian was becoming twitchy from the confinement. He was setting her on edge. He never could stay inside for long.

"You up for a little walk? Stretch our legs for a bit?" He asked Raya.

"Is that wise?" Ortega asked, looking up from her laptop.

He held up their linked wrists, giving the cuffs a jiggle.

"Ian." She said removing her glasses, face intent. "If Ms. Burns wishes to rid herself of you in that dense forest. She could do it. We both read her file. And while I would go after you and haul her ass back here. I don't want to have to go out into those blackfly infested woods."

Raya couldn't stop the laugh that escaped her. Despite herself, she was beginning to like agent Ortega. "She's right." She said to Ian, turning her attention to his face. She was nearly taken aback by the intensity of his gaze.

"Would you?"

"Depends." She couldn't seem to help the breathless reaction either. She realized she actually didn't want to rid herself of Ian. Even though she had work to do, every particle of her wanted Ian to be part of it. It was like the heart ache and anger of the betrayal between them was beginning to dissipate.

"On?"

On? Oh right.

"If you promise to make more scones." She said the first thing that came to mind to set him at ease.

He lifted a brow. "Clothed or not?"

Ian. Naked. She swallowed.

"Okay, I don't need to hear this." Ortega said. "Just don't make me come looking for you."

Ortega was armed and kept her distance from Raya in case she forced her to use her weapon.

Raya had already decided to bide her time. At least until they got down off the mountain and she could get out of the cuffs without maiming anyone.

She knew that was why they cuffed her to Ian in the first place. She might think twice about hurting him, whereas severing anyone else's limb for freedom might be a price she'd quickly pay.

"Not." She challenged, sweeping him with her eyes.

If she was going to escape, she may as well make it easier.

She was rewarded with his slow grin.

"Ian." Ortega said. "Be careful."

Ian nodded to her as he stood.

The woods surrounding the cabin had a magical, primitive quality to them. Alive in a way that was wholly distinct from the wilderness around the lake, where people dwelled all the time.

They walked a little distance through trees, following a narrow trail. Trees were marked at regular intervals, unlike the forest the previous day, where she'd struck Ian in an attempt to escape. Despite all her skills, escaping hand cuffs wasn't one of them. A problem to be dealt with during her next bout of leisure time.

Breathing deeply, she eased her guard. Then she reached out with her magic, seeking a water source.

"There's nothing up here." Ian said.

"A girl has to try."

He snorted.

"I forgot you could sense my magic."

"So did I." He glanced at her.

The trail curled around the rocky surface as it gently descended. The birdsong was deafening as the sun rose higher, peeking through the tree tops above them. The terrain began to fall away on one side.

They rounded another boulder and the trail opened to a cliff top view.

Raya gasped.

They overlooked a vast valley; a rolling carpet of trees.

It reminded her of the old days, together. When they spent days hiking through the woods around one of Ian's lakes. Including this one.

She looked down at their cuffed wrists, side by side. She brushed the back of her hand against his. She felt his attention on her as she looked up into his face. This was the first time they'd been alone in nearly a decade. Stubble shaded his cheeks and jaw, somehow making his lips look softer.

She licked hers, desperately wanting to taste him.

Drawn to her mouth, his gaze caressed her.

She slid her fingers along his palm, inviting his grasp.

Fingers linked, palm to palm, she stepped toward him.

He watched her face as she moved closer.

The air fizzled between them, sending tingles across the flesh of her chest and belly.

She pushed through it until she stood, her breasts a breath from his chest.

So close.

She thought of the previous night. Sleeping with her back to his front. Delicious fantasies of his body moving against hers pebbled her nipples and dampened her panties.

She recalled how well he knew her body, and she knew his.

Glancing down the thin space between them, she lifted her hand to his chest. It was still a solid wall of warm muscle as it rose and fell with each breath beneath her palm. His free hand curled over hers, covering his heart. He leaned over her, lips close to her ear.

"It's still yours."

His whispered brogue ripped through her, slamming her throat, her heart and her core.

The tip of his nose ghosted along the shell of her ear down to the soft, vulnerable flesh below it.

Oh. Oh, he was *so* working her.

And she relished it.

She tilted her head, offering her throat to him as she stepped into his space, pressing her body to his, completing the connection.

An instant later, she found herself pinned with her back to a massive tree, their cuffed hands pressed to the bark over her head.

Ian's free hand gripped her thigh, pulling it up over his hip. She could feel his desire pressed to her hot center.

Dear Goddess, she wanted him to fill her. Wanted him to remind what it was to feel whole again. To feel like a woman full of desire.

She remembered what she was like, before she'd shut herself down.

Her insides throbbed as she wantonly lifted her hips, wrapping her leg around him and drawing him closer still.

Ian could never be close enough.

She slid her free hand along his back, slipped into his jeans, and gripped his ass.

"Ray." He warned, face close to hers. Nose tip to tip. They inhaled each other's breaths.

"It's been so long," she whispered, brushing her lips across his. Her tongue darted out, tasting him. Her hand slid from his ass to grip his hard cock. "Much, much, too long."

His chest rumbled with a deep growl, his body rigid as he struggled for self-control.

She was so ready for him.

Her hand slid up and down his length.

Taunting. Daring. Encouraging.

His body jerked against her.

He forced his eyes open, looking into hers. The sun made them glow like highly polished mahogany.

"Here? Now?"

She nodded. "Yes, now, Ian. Right now."

She craved the security of his body, the connection with him. To not be so alone. Just for a little while.

They helped free each other of their pants in seconds. Then she was guiding his tip to her hot wet core.

She drew a breath of anticipation.

He remained a moment longer nestled between her moist folds.

She tilted her hips so that his crown was at her entrance.

He thrust home.

She cried out.

Home.

They stood as they were. Her back against the trunk of the ancient tree, his face buried in the crook of her neck. Chest to chest in this wild place on a mountain top. The drop to a rolling valley just feet away from where they stood.

Glancing up into the lattice of tree branches, tears filled her vision.

It's still yours

Regardless, she wouldn't ask Ian to be hers again, though she never stopped loving him. Even through her sense of betrayal and anger. She never stopped.

"Fuck me, Ian." Her voice was soft in her demand.

He lifted his head, looking straight into her eyes.

"Hard."

He claimed her mouth and as his tongue swiped hers, he thrust hard, as she'd asked him to.

Her legs wrapped over his hips, the tree bark bit into her back through her shirt.

She relished it as he pumped into her over and over. Relentless.

Raya held on tighter and tighter, desperate for the closeness of his body, his essence.

She'd missed him so damned much.

She crested.

As deep as he was within her, it wasn't enough.

He kept going until she crested again. He followed her into the abyss.

TWELVE

Jean-Guy LeVoleur walked the length of his hotel suite, hands clasped behind his back. The television on the wall was set to the local news. He'd made the three-hour drive from Quebec City to Montreal in anticipation of the meeting with the Ashray and his nephew Charles.

He glanced at the time in the corner of the newscast then to his silent phone on the hotel room desk.

She should have checked in by now.

Something was wrong. He could feel it in his gut. She had a reputation of flawless job executions.

No doubt Charles fucked things up. He snorted and turned back to the large windows overlooking the old quarter near the waterfront. It wasn't as beautiful as his city. It lacked...elegance.

The sooner he could go back the better, though he knew he needed to be here himself to complete the job he'd hired her to do.

It was too important. There was too much on the line.

The door swung open to admit his personal assistant.

"What is it, Marie-Ange?"

"No reports yet, just messages from your contacts. They're expecting the next shipment from your sector in a few days."

He nodded. He'd already delayed things by a week. He couldn't hold off for much longer.

He needed to secure the operation before taking the next usual steps.

And that all depended on Charles.

Jean-Guy needed access to his apartment before he moved ahead. He had to handle this discretely or his whole sector of the ring could fall because of his nephew's sentimental stupidity. What could he do? Charles was his sister's kid.

If he were anyone else...

Anyone else wouldn't be a problem; he'd just deal with them. Simple.

Charles complicated things for him. Immeasurably.

Dealing with Charles required incredible patience, if he was to be entrusted with his entire legacy. With no children of his own, Jean-Guy needed to ensure the survival of the business in the family. Charles was the only choice. He just needed a little more time to mature. More time to understand the way of things.

He sighed and paced the length of the windows, staring out at the gray buildings, gray sky, and gray river front.

He was so close.

"*Merde.*" Jean-Guy swore, glancing at his watch again.

Charles.

Where the hell was the Ashray now? Where was Charles?

Jean-Guy's heart pounded in his chest and his skin flushed. He drew a deep breath.

Calm.

IAN'S GAZE RETURNED TO Raya across the table.

They faced each other over a Scrabble board they'd found tucked away in a cupboard. She was seventeen points ahead in their third game.

In the forest, spent, they'd righted each other's clothing with still more lingering touches before returning to the monotony of the cabin.

He couldn't get enough of her.

They had so much history and yet, there was so much heartache between them, too.

Could she let it go? Could he?

He'd already decided he no longer wanted to hold onto the past. This, with Raya, was different.

They'd hurt each other deeply. Equally.

When he was truthful with himself, he'd never let her go. He'd meant it when he said his heart was still hers.

She'd invited him into her sweet body again. What of her own heart?

Ian wanted all of her.

Words filled the board while the air was silent.

Ana was curled up with a book from the small collection stored with the board games and cards.

Ian never would have figured Odson to be the board games and books type. He supposed everyone got bored in isolation.

He didn't mind it—not when Raya shared it.

It was temporary, he knew. And that was fine with him.

He was thankful she hadn't taken advantage of his vulnerability in the forest to escape. Especially considering how messy the cuffs would have made it.

He glanced up at her again.

Would she try again, as soon as they were free of each other?

No doubt.

Their fucking hadn't changed the fact that she was on a mission.

He straightened and drew a breath, considering the letter tiles in front of him, as he considered his choices for the future.

He'd promised to help her discover the fate of her brother.

He'd admitted his heart was still hers.

Raya had accepted neither his help nor his heart.

He cleared his throat and chose his last few playable tiles and slid them into the spaces between words Raya had placed, launching him several points ahead of her.

It didn't matter.

She was too important to him to withdraw his support and love from her now. He realized that in the last few years. He wasn't going to fuck up another opportunity. Whether she realized it or not, when they worked together, they were both the richer for it. He knew that now.

She placed her last tile, finishing the game and tying the score.

The rest of the afternoon and evening passed in a cloud of quiet riffs of conversation, tea, and little things to fill the time until the hour grew late again.

"I'll wash up the dishes." Ana said with a yawn.

"Why don't you bed down; we can do it." Raya said.

Ana's perfect brows rose as she looked from Raya to Ian, who nodded and stood to collect the abandoned cups and plates from the table.

"Go on, then," he said, reaching for the still warm kettle to use for the washing up. Without running water, they'd had to get creative, like in the old days before indoor plumbing.

"Alright. I won't be far if you need anything." She said, heading for the couch.

Dishes washed and set aside, Raya followed Ian out of the screen door to dump the water from the bowl they'd used.

"It's perfect up here." Raya said, face upturned toward the stars and wisps of space dust visible between the overhead crowns of oak and maple.

Ian set the bowl aside and joined her in a few moments of stargazing.

"I've often thought about the many nights we spent together, just like this." Her chest rose and fell. "Those were good days."

"They were."

She turned toward him. "I can't go back, Ian."

"I know."

"I wish things were different but-"

"I understand."

The rest of her words died on her tongue as she looked into his face, seeing that he truly did. Her free hand rose up, her fingertips gently traced the bruises she made. "I'm sorry."

"Nothing to apologize for." He kissed her palm. The memory of her flying fists and feet still stung, more his pride than anything else.

There'd no doubt been a flowing water source in the valley. She could have fought, again, for her freedom, despite the cuffs. She hadn't. Instead, she'd invited him into her.

"You've certainly learned how to protect yourself."

Her laugh was short. "You have no idea."

His eyes narrowed on her, his gut rolling over. He could imagine. He recalled what people were like. And diving into the underworld as she'd done...

Dropping his gaze to their cuffed hands, he slid his fingers between hers, which in turn tightened on his. "We should get some sleep too."

They didn't know what would come the following day.

He nodded and retrieved the bowl on their way back inside.

Ana was curled into a ball, wedged in the corner of the couch. Ian paused to adjust the throw that had slipped from her shoulder before going into the bedroom with Raya.

Raya closed the door and slipped the lock.

Ian's gaze snapped to her face.

Her eyes were trained on his, in the darkness of the room.

She reached for the hem of her shirt and pulled it up over her head, letting it drop to the chain of the cuffs tethering them. Then she reached for his before unbuttoning her pants and letting them drop to the floor. His joined hers as his gaze swept her perfect body. Full breasts and hips, muscled thighs and strong toned arms were testament to the hard hours of physical training she must have endured over the years. Her fingers slid with gentle familiarity over his taut abdomen, making his dick jerk with need.

She licked her lips, stepping closer. He grew harder.

She was so fucking beautiful. He wanted nothing more than to slide into her hot wet channel.

First, he needed to worship her.

This could very well be the last time she welcomed his touch.

Dipping his head, his lips brushed the tops of her breasts. Her head fell back with a sigh. With his free hand, his fingers ghosted her spine till he found the clasp of her bra.

He was rewarded with a groan as his mouth closed over first one peaked nipple, then the other.

His arm slid around her hips as he turned their bodies so that he could back her toward the bed. He followed her as she eased back onto the mattress. Staring down into her face, her gray eyes were luminous in the moonlight streaming in through the window.

So beautiful.

He kissed her with all the gentleness in his soul until she parted her lips and invited him in.

His tongue swept hers.

She groaned, her free hand clasping his back, nails gliding along his skin. With each plunge of his tongue, his cock throbbed with need.

He wasn't going to just fuck her this time.

He had years to make up for.

Neither of them knew what the dawn would bring.

With reluctance he relinquished her mouth and made his way down her body.

Throat, collarbone, breasts. The curve of her belly button, hip, and inner thigh.

Hooking his fingers under edge of her panties, he slid them down her legs so that she was fully exposed to his gaze.

Beautiful.

He sought to devour more of her.

He licked and nibbled.

She gasped and sighed.

Her fingers slid along his jaw. "Hold me."

He kissed her wrist, then her soft skin just above her core, working his way back up to her mouth, turning her so that she was cradled in his arms. With her smooth back pressed to his chest, his cock rested along the cleft of her lovely bottom.

He kissed her nape, teeth grazing the sensitive flesh below the delicate shell of her ear. Their fingers were intertwined as his hand moved over her breasts.

Her gasps made him pulse.

Hands still linked, and ignoring the fabric draped from their wrists, she guided his hand down to the apex of her thighs, sliding each of their middle fingers into her hot channel.

She was ready. So fucking ready for him.

Tilting her hips, her arse rubbed against his cock, making it buck.

As she hooked her ankle over his calf, he aligned himself, their fingers moving away to make room for him.

He slid into her.

This time he gave her an inch with each slow flick of his fingertip on her nub until he was fully buried within her.

She turned her head so that she looked at him over the curve of her shoulder, lids heavy with need. "Ian." She said, her fingers gripping his harder.

He took his time, no matter how much his body craved a quick release. It screamed at him to pump and slam.

He resisted.

Savor.

His mouth claimed hers again.

With each slow swipe of his tongue against hers, he slid out to the tip and in to the hilt.

Her soft gasps and moans became sharper, breathier, until he knew she was almost there.

One last thrust of his tongue and his cock and she was coming so hard, her grip on him was a painful bittersweet haze, forcing him to surge even deeper into her, their palms cradling their joined sexes, holding on to the moment.

When thought returned, he lifted his forehead from her shoulder and looked at her. Her face was turned to his, her eyes large and luminous in the moonlight.

He could see the unshed tears. The words remained unspoken between them.

But he knew.

He knew she still loved him.

THIRTEEN

RAYA WAS LOST IN her thoughts, staring in the general direction of the brunch dishes on the table. Across from Ian again; she was almost growing used to the cuffs that still linked their wrists.

The familiarity was lulling.

Her body had responded to that familiarity, pulling her heart along with it. Her brain had to get things in order. Regardless of the fact that Ian was right here with her and he'd apologized for the past, she still had work to do.

She had to find out what happened to Dominique. That's what *all* of this was about.

And she was finally on the cusp.

Get to Jean-Guy LeVoleur via Chuck. LeVoleur was the head of one of the transportation sectors. If she could get close to him, get his trust, she could gain access to his business information. That's what the *Organization* needed. She also needed to find clues that would lead her to her brother. She just *knew* it was all connected. Every step taken to find him had led her in this direction.

Her heart twisted. She should never have left him alone. He was far too gentle.

She grimaced. There was a time she'd been gentle too. Soft. Impressionable. She glanced at Ian. He stared at her with that unique intensity that touched her heart and made her belly flutter.

The distinct sound of an engine pulled everyone's attention from brunch and from each other.

Ana downed the last of her coffee and went out to meet Agent Perenga.

Raya looked across the table at Ian. He was still studying her closely.

"Agent Carson Perenga." She said.

Ian's brow rose.

"He's a good friend?"

"We go back many years."

"Long before you and I met? I've never heard you mention him before."

Ian shrugged and pushed his empty dish aside. "He's been busy working for the Global Paranormal Security Agency, saving paranormals from other paranormals. And humans from paranormals."

"Not your thing."

He shook his head.

"Until now."

He sipped his coffee. His eyes lingered on her face before he spoke. "I believed in fate, back in the days when we were happy, you and I. Then I lost that belief when we fell apart. Lately, the quiet life hasn't been enough. Not for a long time."

His words made her heart drop. She turned her mug between her palms. Sunlight streaming in from the kitchen window glinted off the cuffs that still linked their wrists.

Agent Perenga still had the key.

When he unlocked them, would she still slip away? Her eyes slid from the cuffs to Ian's face. His remained on her face, his expression guarded.

"And now?"

"Fate? I dinnae know." He cleared his throat.

Raya's heart skipped a beat at the slip of his natural brogue. For a moment, as she stared at him, the emotion in his eyes was raw. He blinked, then sipped his coffee like they were discussing travel plans.

She couldn't explain it either.

It was uncanny, that the one time he stepped outside his usual anti-people attitude to help his friend, they were sent crashing into one another again after all these years. What did it mean—if anything?

"He's trustworthy?"

"Carson? Yeah. All about doing what's right."

"What about his superiors?"

"Jack Maeda is good folk. I've known him a long time too. And he reports to Joey Kane."

"I've heard of her." She nodded. "And who does she report to?"

Ian shrugged. "How should I know? What does it matter?"

"Exactly. You don't know. And it does matter. A lot."

"They're all working toward protecting everyone. Humans as well as paranormals."

"And somewhere in that chain, someone may be exploiting the system."

"You think the GPSA is compromised?"

"I didn't say that...but I don't know for sure. Could be somewhere above GPSA's umbrella."

She twisted her mug between her palms again, tracing the rim with her thumb.

Options. Risks.

She glanced back up at Ian's handsome face.

Complications.

Several days of stubble coated his jaw and cheeks. The deep-seated memory of the sensation of that stubble grazing over her body, so many years ago...and along her throat just a few hours ago, sprang to the forefront of her thoughts, sending a shiver rippling through her.

She huffed and shoved it away.

Distractions.

She had to focus on her job. On finding Dominique.

FINALLY.

She was getting somewhere. The Ashray's defenses were finally lowered long enough that Analiese could get a reading on her.

She'd made it pretty frikking hard. She was so damned guarded.

Now, Ana could at least pick through the images and impressions enough to create a very rough picture from the fractured pieces.

The second Ian and the Ashray had walked through the cabin door the day before, she could feel the sexual energy fill the small space. Sensual satisfaction. It rolled over and through her like a tidal wave, triggering her own desires, best quickly locked away again.

Focus.

This job was important to Raya Burns because she believed it was somehow connected to something else...her brother's disappearance? She couldn't detect any other underlying motive.

It was the clearest and strongest impression she'd been able to pick up since she'd started trying to read the woman. Ana was exhausted from trying to be 'on' all this time to glean the slightest subconscious information.

There was also not a whiff of a doubt that the woman still had very deep-rooted feelings for Ian and she was incredibly conflicted by this. It was also clear that the longer she was with him, the weaker her guard became.

Until Carson drove up.

The sound of his closing car door had been a trigger switch and the Ashray's walls slammed back in place.

Ana went to meet Carson outside.

She doesn't trust us.

Well, we'll just have to find a way to get her to.

Carson closed the last few steps. "Good morning."

Ana nodded. "Coffee? We still have some in the pot."

"Any luck with our new friend?"

"Some." She relayed the little she'd been able to glean from Raya.

Carson nodded, thoughtful. "I've been talking to Maeda and Kane."

"This is serious."

"Yes. It's big."

Ana raised a brow. "The feeling I'm getting from you is disturbing."

"Don't do that. And yes, it is disturbing." He blew out a breath. She could see he was as tired as the rest of them were.

"Sorry. I've been *on* for so long now, I'm picking up everything. Has Lirikai reported in?"

He nodded. "She's good."

"That's a relief."

"We need to get her to work with us." He said with a nod toward the cabin.

A grunt escaped Ana. "We're going to have to find a damned good angle. But I think we may be able to. I'm getting a clearer picture of what's under all that steeliness." Ana sighed, turning to regard the saggy cabin. They both stared at the hovel-like dwelling. No one would ever guess just how deceiving the outside was compared to what lay within. Once you get past that outer layer, there was so much going on inside.

Ana's ability sort of worked that way. She had to see past the exterior and get a sense of what was really inside for the true story. What and how things were compartmentalized, how strong those divisions were, how deep the foundations went.

"Come and grab what's left of the coffee and Ian's scones." Ana said, heading back toward the door.

Carson nodded and followed her. "I'm always up for one of Ian's scones."

As she held the door for him to enter, she had the sense that he was holding back something. Something important. Her gut tightened, hoping that whatever it was, it wasn't going to throw their progress sideways.

"Time to take you back down the mountain." Carson said to Raya.

Analiese noted that the stiffness of her posture and mask-like expression returned.

One step forward, two steps back. Ana swallowed a sigh and poured the last of the coffee into a mug for Carson, then went to get her small bag. They left the remainder of the supplies they'd brought up to the cabin.

Downing the coffee, Carson locked up the cabin and everyone filed into the car. No one really said much. Ana sat up front with Carson, still trying to glean energy from Raya and sometimes from Ian.

She could feel their emotions. She could sense their desire for each other, which was almost overwhelming. And the deep, deep longing.

It was so strong. And yet, to look at them, they were a pair of strangers occupying the back seat of the car.

She continued to concentrate on their emotions as Carson drove.

Ian slid his fingers alongside Raya's on the seat between them. The tip of her little finger stroked his, then went still. She didn't pull away.

As soon as their car reached the main road, Ana called Lirikai for directions to where they would meet.

Once at the meet point, Carson pinned a wary eye on Raya as he unlocked the cuffs binding her to Ian. "Ian, I want you to go talk to Lirikai. Raya will stay with us."

Ana moved into their line of view with a hand on her taser, her eyes glued to Raya's face.

Ian nodded and headed for Lirikai's car with a glance in Raya's direction. She wasn't looking at him. She'd kept her gaze averted from him since Carson arrived to collect them from the cabin.

"Meduse is still somewhere in this lake." Lirikai said to Ian as he got into the car. "I followed his scent along the banks for a long time before he started crossing back and forth."

"Was he looking for something?" Carson asked.

She shrugged. "Maybe food or clothes? His scent is heavy with desperation."

"There are campsites everywhere on both sides of the lake, he should have been able to steal something by now."

"He probably has, to have gotten this far." She turned in her seat to look at Ian full on. "I don't like this guy. He hasn't hurt anyone yet, but when people get desperate, they give up or get violent."

Ian nodded. "The sooner we catch him the better, obviously."

"Yes. We need him to get to his boss. As your Ashray is doing. This man is the small jellyfish." Her lips quirked. "We want the bigger jellyfish."

"You want me to help Raya get to him?"

"It's risky. We could just follow them. Carson prefers to have her cooperation."

He nodded. "Well, you're going to have to find something she really wants. She wants to know what happened to her brother. Can you get that?"

"We're working on it, but it isn't easy. Disappearance cases are hard to solve for a reason. We want you to find out everything you can from her."

"Right."

When he signed up for the job, he was helping Carson find a runaway prisoner, not interacting with the lost love of his life, who'd completely changed from the woman he'd known, only to dive headlong into a crime syndicate case.

I don't know her anymore. He had to keep reminding himself.

Did he ever?

He thought he did at one time. He was clearly wrong.

He'd had an idea of who she was—a soft, delicate, beautiful woman that had been treated very badly. A woman that just wanted to live life in peace. Like him. And he'd thought he'd be the man to shelter and protect her from the world, in the sanctuary of his lakes, far, far from the insanity of humanity.

He hadn't taken it seriously when she'd said she wanted to know what happened when her brother disappeared. He really hadn't. He'd thought her mother was pushing on her to use her ability to find out, and she was doing it out of a sense of family loyalty and guilt.

Maybe she was. Ian didn't know. Whatever it was, it was enough to drive her in a direction he certainly never would have thought she, of all people, would go.

A mercenary working in the underworld.

It was an incredible leap.

She clearly was not the woman he'd thought she was.

And yet the familiarity of their bond tugged at him. It pulled at his flesh. It triggered memories of their time together. Another lifetime together. Another world, one he had believed long dead.

Their bodies certainly still responded to one another. Thought and emotion were far more complicated than the simplicity of a familiar touch.

Could there be a new world? A new lifetime for them with new memories to be made? He thought of the previous night. Their bodies knew each other, as did their magic.

Did he still want her? Physically, yes—always.

He said he'd help her find her brother. And he would do what he could, but that was different from trying to breathe life into something that she wasn't interested in rekindling.

FOURTEEN

"We want you to work with us."

Raya stared at Agent Perenga's face. "Of course you do."

His lips compressed.

They were standing outside the car. She could have made a run for it, might even have made it. Move in, take down Ortega before she could draw her Taser, and then round on Perenga.

She'd have to be damned fast. She held back.

She wanted to know where this was going before she did.

The Agent had clearly wanted her cooperation from the time they'd found her at the hospital until now.

That old glimmer of hope for help. The one she'd given up on after law enforcement had repeatedly turned her away during her search for Dominique.

"What are you offering?"

"I told you, we want the same thing you do."

She shrugged. "What are you offering?" she repeated, crossing her arms.

"Support."

She quirked a brow.

Her attention was drawn to the other car that Lirikai and Ian were emerging from.

"And my *record*?"

He drew in a deep breath. "My bosses have agreed to ignore it, *if* you work for us."

"I told you, I'm already working for-"

"Yes, I know, a hidden group. Deeper than the GPSA. I've been caught up. And my superiors are reaching out to them to confirm your claims. Until then..." He shrugged.

Raya felt the color drain from her face. If they knew she'd been caught by GPSA and there was a leak somewhere, this could affect everything she had worked for. She needed to be seen as capable and unbending.

"If anyone finds out I've been caught, the whole operation will be compromised."

"No one will. Maeda and Kane are discrete."

She needed an impeccable image to continue to move along the underground channels that she'd spent years gaining access to.

The heat from Ian's body rolled toward her as he stepped into the space beside her

"Once you find Chuck and help him get this valuable thing his boss wants, you're going to be delivering it?"

She nodded.

"We want to bring him in."

"I need him." She snapped.

"To get information about what happened to your brother." Carson acknowledged.

She glared at him, then nodded.

"We'll provide support when you go in to complete the job."

"Raid his place."

"We can find it if you help us tap and track." Ortega said.

"What makes you think this would work?"

"You have a reputation of impeccable success. He knows you deliver. That's why he hired you. There's no reason to suspect you wouldn't."

"As long as he doesn't know I've lost Chuck. He is the key." Her teeth ground together at the thought of her failure.

"Well, lucky for you, Lirikai has been tracking him all this time. Ian knows the lake better than anyone, so he'll get you to Chuck. We'll all be keeping an eye on you."

Raya wasn't expecting the sense of relief that overwhelmed her. Tears stung her eyes. She turned her face away from the others. Looking at the visible expanse of Lake Champlain, she blinked and ham-fisted her emotions into a state of control.

She took a deep breath. The lake was beautiful. Ian's lake. She didn't want to think about the time they'd spent here together, which didn't seem like long enough—even then. He had a cabin of his own nestled on a rise overlooking an inlet near the deepest part of the lake. It couldn't be far from here.

Could she trust them?

Her brain screamed to ditch them as soon as possible, get the job done, get the information needed from the mob boss and get the hell out and on her way.

Could she get the information? She had planned for much more time spent working for the man, gaining access to his compound, infiltrating his systems. More spying and sneaking. For how long?

If—*if*—GPSA were really going to help, it could be an easy way out. A quicker way to get to the information she craved most. The fate of her brother. To know if he was alive or dead. If he was alive, then she had to find him. If he was dead, then she needed to find a way to bring closure and peace to her soul after accepting her failure. Her failure to protect him.

She glanced at the agents, all staring at her. Waiting. Then she looked at Ian. She couldn't read his expression. There was tension in his full lips. She recognized the signs of his inner conflict.

He said he'd help her find her brother.

It was a long shot.

Turning her attention back to Agent Perenga, she drew a breath. "Anything you find in that compound, I want access to it. Even if I do find information about my brother, my work doesn't end there. I'm committed to doing what I can to break this trafficking ring. They've taken so many people, and have no intention of stopping any time soon. I know too much to walk away. Seen too much."

Ian frowned.

Perenga reached out a hand. "Deal. Welcome to the GPSA."

She shook his hand, then Lirikai's. Ortega's gaze slid from her to Ian then back again. She too, extended her hand.

Raya hesitated before taking it.

Fortune teller.

At this point, she no longer had anything left to hide. She shook Ortega's delicate hand.

At the contact, Ortega's hand clenched on hers, then her eyes rolled back in her head and she tipped backwards.

Perenga caught her. "Analiese?" His voice was harsh with concern.

"Put her in the car." Lirikai said, opening the door.

Perenga slid Ortega's slight frame onto the leather seat, easing her head against the headrest. "She'll be alright. It's happened before. We just have to wait for her to come around." He said, straightening. "You two better get going. Lirikai will catch you up."

CHUCK MEDUSE WAS SERIOUSLY rethinking his brilliant plan to sting and ditch the Ashray bitch.

He hated being told what to do—by anyone.

He'd had to do something.

She was taking him to his uncle, after retrieving something from his place.

She didn't know what he had to retrieve. That was good.

That also meant that he needed to get there as soon as possible.

Uncle Jean-Guy knew.

Fear gripped his gut. Chuck was his nephew. He didn't believe *he* was in any danger. If he were anyone else, there'd be a puddle of piss soaking his feet, but he was family.

What the Ashray didn't know, was that the 'something' was actually a 'someone.'

Someone Chuck was desperate to protect from his uncle.

Maybe he'd been too hasty in ditching the Ashray. Maybe he should have followed her plan, used her resources to get back.

An outdoorsy guy, Chuck was not.

And just maybe, he might have been able to talk her into helping him instead of doing the job his uncle had hired her for.

He scratched that thought. She had a reputation of getting the job done. His uncle wouldn't have hired her otherwise.

Fuck. He stared at the shoreline, watching vacationers enjoy the water.

He needed to get out of the water. The fresh river water was wrong for his shifted self. He needed salt water to survive long periods off land.

He had no clothes or other supplies. He'd slept naked in some bushes shivering all damned night, with no one around from whom he could easily steal what he needed.

The Ashray had made it exceedingly clear just how much he needed to keep his face hidden. Even out here, people had access to the news and could recognize the escaped convict.

He moved on, heading north through the water.

Why this way? Why didn't his uncle just leave a boat for them somewhere or send a driver for them? He could have had men pick them up anywhere outside the prison.

What was the deal?

Something was going on with him.

Was he trying to break him down? Make him desperate? It was fucking working.

He obviously had a strong enough reason to go through the effort of hiring the Ashray to break him out of prison.

At first, Chuck had thought it was because he was family. Maybe his uncle had a soft spot for him. More likely a favor to his mother. Then the Ashray had mentioned his secret place in Montreal and picking something up from there.

No. It was self-preservation. Uncle Jean-Guy wanted to ensure his position was safe. And the person Chuck had hidden at his place was a threat.

Chuck's heart hammered in his chest. He could take some comfort in knowing that his uncle obviously had not yet found what he was looking for. Chuck had to get back as soon as possible, and find another safe place to stay. The question was, why now? After all these years, why now? How did he find out Chuck had deceived him?

He had to think. And that was hard to do when you were exhausted, cold and hungry.

He eyed the boats docked nearby.

It would be easy to steal one.

It was also the fastest way to give away his position if he were seen, too—as the Ashray had also mentioned.

Steal a boat and get there faster. Steal a boat and get caught.

He continued upstream. He would decide when it was dark. Hopefully, he'd be able to come across some supplies. He was getting so damned hungry it was hard to think straight.

FIFTEEN

RAYA STARED, UNSEEING, AT the passing landscape.

Ian directed Lirikai as she drove to a local marina and they secured a boat rental. She told them where she'd last seen Chuck's floating iridescent bladder. It was early enough in the day that lake traffic was minimal.

Lirikai handed Raya's backpack and knife to Ian.

"Ana will be okay?" Ian asked her.

She shrugged. "Carson said she would. I haven't seen her pass out like that before, but I don't know her as well as he does." She dropped the rental key into his palm. "Good luck," she said to him, then turned to Raya. Lirikai handed her a small device which she recognized as a tracker. "If you fuck us over, I'll come for you myself."

Raya bristled at the threat. "You really think you-"

"Come on, we're wasting time." Ian pulled her arm toward the docks.

"I don't take threats lightly, Ian."

"Barra'kidai don't threaten, they promise."

"I don't give a shit what she is."

"Get in the boat."

She cast a baleful look in Lirikai's direction. She stood watching them from beside the car.

"I don't like her."

"You don't have to. Let's go. You drive, and as soon as we get far enough out, I'll go in and start searching for him. If he follows the currents, he could be among the islands." He dropped Raya's belongings into the boat.

Raya started the engine and they were soon headed for the center of the lake. They passed several fishermen and an anchored sailboat.

She cut the engine. Ian immediately began stripping down.

She couldn't help herself.

As his shirt came up over his head, exposing his well-defined abs, her mouth watered. Her tongue had explored every one of those ridges and valleys. His jeans sagged on his hips, the belt slung far below his bellybutton. Her fingers itched to slip into the loose gap.

"Ray?" His low voice snapped her back. "You okay?"

She blinked and huffed. "Yeah, fine. Thinking."

Focus, Raya. We have work to do.

"I have a cache of supplies stashed toward the end of the lake. Chuck's going to need something to wear once we find him."

He assessed her as he slipped his shoes and socks off. "Okay, meet me back around here."

She should look away. Watch for boaters or folks along the banks. Her eyes slid back to Ian.

Focus.

She licked her lips. Her fingers twitched, drawn to his warm flesh again.

When they'd been together, neither could go long without touching the other.

His jeans hit the bottom of the boat and her panties were suddenly damp.

Raya groaned, low in her throat.

She'd buried the memories of how beautiful his body was. Tall, muscled, with graceful proportions. His tanned skin was coated with a light dusting of fine hair that caught the sunlight.

She turned away from him, gripping the steering wheel of the boat to stop herself from reaching for him.

The boat rocked gently, followed by a light splash.

She drew a deep breath, knowing he was in the water.

Releasing the steering wheel, she moved to the edge of the boat. He glanced up at her before letting himself sink below the surface of the water. She watched his pale, wavering form sink into the darkness of the lake.

At the same time the water rippled unnaturally, her flesh tingled.

He was shifting below the surface.

She'd forgotten that her magic recognized his too. A funny little thing. When they were close to one another and one shifted the other could feel it.

She felt as though she'd been punched in the heart.

She'd never felt that connected to anyone else. Her connection with her brother was different. So much...thinner.

A form, lighter in color compared to the lakebed, rose up under the boat. She recognized Ian's head and long neck gliding under the boat. Soon the mass of his powerful body slid past as well and narrowed again to the pointed tip of his tail.

She cranked the starter of the boat and gunned the engine, avoiding the area above where she could make out his shape, and headed for the cache.

He'd be scenting the water, given how small and hard to see Chuck was. He'd be next to impossible to find and she wasn't sure if Ian's sonar hearing could pick up a delicate mass like Chuck's jellyfish form.

The pack was exactly where she'd left it, hidden among thick brush not far from the mouth of the Richelieu River. It didn't appear as though it had been disturbed since she'd placed it there weeks ago.

This job had been so long in the planning. It was nearly done.

Drawing a deep breath, she retrieved the bag and got back into the boat, tossing it next to the one she already had.

Could she trust that the GPSA agents would come through and back her up?

They wanted the same thing she did.

Would they arrest her when the time came? Round her up with the others? If that happened, would the *Organization* bail her out, or cut their ties to maintain their anonymity?

At this point she wasn't sure she cared so long as she got the information she needed about her brother.

She was tired, trying to keep from drowning in the murk of the world she'd submerged herself into.

As driven as she was to complete this mission she'd tasked herself with, she longed for the simple life she'd shared with Ian. Maybe, when she had her answers....

Raya was getting closer. So close. She could feel it.

The wind scrubbed her face and whipped through her hair as she sped the boat back to where she'd left Ian.

From the moment they'd been given the news of Dominique's likely death by ocean suicide, there'd been an underlying current of heaviness in her gut. She hadn't been surprised that he'd been reported missing. He'd disappeared from the face of the earth. Swallowed by the sea, they'd told her. In her heart, she hadn't believed it. The vibrating tension of an invisible cord that bound her to her little brother remained. It was like a precise, maintained music note that hadn't cut or faded completely. She was going to find out the truth, one way or another.

As she looked out over the expanse of the lake visible to her, she considered what Ian had said to her all those years ago.

Denial.

He'd said that she was holding onto childhood memories of someone who was no longer the child she knew. Maybe, but neither was she the child she once was. At her core—and his too—there was still that part of both of them that was. It didn't matter that it was buried deep below the layers of life experiences.

This is what her gut was telling her, or perhaps her wishful thinking.

Maybe she was in denial. This wasn't the first time she'd questioned herself on the matter. And it likely wouldn't be the last.

Her instinct told her to keep searching. So, she did.

She blinked away the sudden onslaught of tears and breathed deeply of the silky air flowing over the lake's surface.

Seeing Ian again—being close to him after all this time—had set her off balance.

She needed to get a grip.

Acknowledge the truth to herself.

She still felt something for him.

She still wanted him.

They were both changed.

Raya huffed. He truly had changed. Something she never thought would happen. He'd been so set in his ways.

His promise of help was like an outstretched hand drawing her up from the depths that she'd sunk to, inviting her to the surface of the living world again.

She still had a job to do, and it was still more important than anything else. That had not changed.

In the boat, she waited, letting the peace of the lake and its surrounding mountains ease her heart.

This was one of Ian's homes.

She'd always understood why he loved it so much. It was another world, and it was so very easy to be lost in it without time.

When her brother had gone missing, she could no longer afford the luxury of existing in the fog of a time and place set apart from the rest of the world.

She was sorry that Ian hadn't been able to understand that.

She straightened, peering over the edge of the boat. His form became visible as he approached. Energy rippled over her as he shifted into his human form. She turned away as he climbed in. Once his jeans were back on, he directed her to where he'd found Chuck.

"Among a cluster of large rocks on the east bank."

She nodded and started the engine for the last time.

"I'M NOT LETTING YOU go alone, Ray," Ian said again.

They'd guided the boat into a small tree-lined inlet and cut the engine, letting it drift closer to the gentle sandy rise.

"You don't have a choice."

Ian stepped closer to her, forcing her to look up into his face.

Ignoring her scowl, he leaned closer, allowing the subtleties of her scent to infuse him.

She wasn't cowed by his looming presence. Instead, she locked her eyes on his.

His mouth quirked at the defiant glint in her beautiful eyes.

"This is how it works, Ian. I do the job. Alone. I'm expected to deliver. Alone. Therefore, I will complete my job as expected. Alone. You tagging along like a little bodyguard would fuck everything up. So stand down." Her voice hardened on the last word.

He blinked. Another reminder of how much she'd changed.

Pride flared in his chest. He'd always known she was strong.

She wasn't hiding it anymore.

His gaze swept her determined face.

"You are so goddamned beautiful." His voice was husky and thick.

Her eyes widened, clearly not expecting those particular words. Then they narrowed again. "I go alone, Ian."

She didn't move when his right hand reached for her. She didn't stop his fingers from sliding up the side of her throat to her jaw or step away when he moved closer still.

He didn't miss the subtle shiver his touch incited.

"I have missed you, these years past." He whispered from his heart.

He eased closer, drawing out the descent of his mouth toward hers, giving her the chance to pull away at any point.

There was a soft fizzle as his lips made contact with hers.

By the next breath, she was pressed to him, her arms around his torso. Her mouth devoured his. She opened to his tongue, welcoming. The familiarity of her sweet taste overwhelmed him. He'd already gone hard at the first touch of her lips, now he swelled painfully for her.

His head reeled with memories of their past lovemaking and the desire to bury himself in her warm body again and again was overwhelming.

He never could get enough of her. Never.

They were supposed to be resuming a chase.

But she was asking him to let her go.

He wanted to remind her of what they'd once had; something beautiful, pure and primal.

He wanted to entice her back to him.

Ian gripped Raya's arse, rocking her hips against his, leaving no doubts about how much he wanted her.

She was just as hot for him. He could feel it through the layers of their jeans.

Her mouth wasn't enough. He wanted to taste more of her sweetness.

His fingers twisted the button of her jeans and eased the zipper down, granting him access to the lace of her panties. A second later, his fingers slid into her core.

Goddess, so was so hot and wet.

She groaned into his mouth.

His fingers slid in and out of her tight channel, his thumb grazing her nub.

"Ian I-" Her breath hitched and she came, gripping and flooding his fingers with her warm honey. Her hands gripped the muscles of his back.

He was so engorged it was painful, but he'd made her come. Fast and hard. Again.

Bittersweet.

He licked her juices from his fingertips.

Her face turned rosy, and he chuckled.

She panted, staring up into his face. The mask was gone and he could read every nuance.

There she was. The Ray he knew, her face alight like the sunshine that warmed them both.

He kissed her. Deep and heartfelt, sinking everything he was into that kiss. He pulled away as slowly as he'd approached her.

He pulled the zipper of her jeans back up and fastened the button. "We're not finished yet." He whispered.

The sound of another boat engine in the distance brought them back to the here and now.

"I'll see you in Montreal." He promised.

With a lingering glance, she got out of the boat, taking her knife and both backpacks, and was soon swallowed by the trees encroaching on the shore of the lake.

SIXTEEN

RAYA STARED AT CHUCK'S tired face.

She focused on that as her body still hummed from Ian's attentions. The moment had been so damned impulsive. She couldn't help letting him touch her. She'd craved it.

On the open lake, everything between them had flooded back; the ease of who they were, together.

It was dangerous accepting him. She'd thought her heart was cold after so many years. It was just dormant, waiting.

She hadn't expected to crest so damned fast; it was embarrassing. It was just another reminder of how much she missed him in her life, and deeply desired him.

And he'd promised more.

She understood what that meant and she couldn't afford to let it distract her from what she needed to do now.

Chuck was fully dressed and they were five minutes into what he thought were negotiations after he'd inhaled a protein bar from the cache pack.

She let him talk.

They really needed to get moving, but this could be fruitful.

As he talked and talked, she schooled her features and posture while her excitement soared.

He was going to make this easy. About fucking time.

Chuck was wrapping up.

Love of his life. Protect them from his uncle.

"Why?"

He shuffled, looking down at his feet.

"If you want me to consider throwing a job, you have to give me the reason—and a substantial amount of money. No bullshit."

He looked up at her with a spark of hope.

In all the time she'd eavesdropped on him in jail, not once had he mentioned someone important to him in that apartment. He had bragged it was his little love nest. The place where the parties happened.

She assumed he'd been bullshitting his prison peers. Was he bullshitting her now?

When she agreed to break him out of prison, she'd assumed LeVoleur wanted her to retrieve an object—money, art, jewels, or even information. A person was much more complicated and expensive. She ground her teeth.

Chuck was exhausted and desperate. He would tell her anything he might think she would bend to.

He drew in a deep breath, eyes trained on her face.

"He was one of the intended merchandises. I pulled him off the ship."

She was not expecting that. He? Now all the prison bullshit about the women and the parties made sense.

"Nicki can place my uncle on that ship. Name some of the other victims, identify his men and some investors. I have absolutely nothing else my uncle could possibly want."

"And this victim is your lover now?" She couldn't hide the incredulous tone from her voice.

He straightened. "We connected."

She swallowed the words on the tip of her tongue, took a breath and counted.

Her mind reeled. This person could be the key she needed to find her brother. Was there a chance he was abducted from the same beach her brother had disappeared from, if the trafficking ring worked the same locations down the coast?

It was a thin chance. Very thin.

"Start walking. Tell me more about this lover of yours and the night you met—where and when, and I'll think about it."

Relief flooded his expression. She didn't miss the tears that sprang to his eyes before he dropped them. "We met at the beach..."

Don't go soft, Raya.

She guided him north.

He kept talking.

He'd been talking all throughout the first leg of their journey, before he'd stung her, but the chatter had been so very different.

A couple of days alone and vulnerable in the wilderness seemed to have done what a couple of months in a state penitentiary hadn't.

She had to think this through.

The mob boss had sent her to break his nephew out of prison, trek him up to Montreal to retrieve something of value from his secret apartment and take both to him at a meeting place to be determined later.

What was she missing?

Why hadn't she been told that this thing of value was a person? Did he know? Was it a guess?

Why hadn't he, as Chuck had whined, provided transportation? She'd assumed it was in order to maintain as low a profile as possible, so that Chuck wouldn't be tracked to the border and to Montreal. Less chance of being seen. Was it punishment for Chuck's betrayal?

She had to focus on her job. Make him disappear from the prison like a ghost. Get Chuck to the meeting place unseen.

She'd deal with LeVoleur's attempt to swindle her later.

She glanced back at Chuck. If he wasn't bullshitting her about this secret rescued lover, which she was deeply skeptical of, maybe—just maybe—Chuck was more of a key to her problems than she had initially realized.

It was going to be damned hard trying to view him from a different perspective.

Or maybe none of his confessions made any difference at all.

ANALIESE CRACKED HER EYES open to the two looming faces of Carson and Lirikai.

Her instincts jerked her body back into the leather of the seat. No matter that she knew them both, having two powerful beasts that close to her was unnerving. Even if they wore human faces, her 'fight-flight-freeze' instinct knew better.

"You gave me a fright, Ana." Carson said, his expression full of concern.

"So did you." She mumbled.

He frowned and eased away from her, giving her space. "I don't like when you do that."

"Pass out? Me either. It's not like I do it on purpose."

He reached for a water bottle that was in the central drink holder and passed it to Ana.

"What happened to you?" Lirikai asked, clearly impatient to get to the point.

"Vision?" Carson asked.

Analiese nodded as she uncapped the bottle and sipped. "Powerful."

"And?" Lirikai prompted.

Ana looked down at the bottle in her hands as she sifted through the images and overwhelming emotions that had crashed over her when she'd touched Raya Burns' hand.

She recalled the clear look of defiance on Burns' face right before blackness had dropped Ana like a stone.

Burns knew what Ana was about to do and she hadn't backed away from it.

She'd opened the gate and given her full access.

Why?

A cry for help? A way of conveying information without breaking her code?

"Well?" Lirikai said.

"I need time to process."

"Talk it out." Carson reached into his pocket to extract his phone and opened the recorder app.

Talk it out, like she did with Maeda. She'd only started talking out the process with Maeda in the last few months, as he helped her strengthen and hone her ability. She wanted to be more useful than just a desk agent coordinating the west coast office. When Carson had called her for this case, she'd jumped at the chance. And so far, all her hard work with Maeda was paying off.

She closed her eyes and started talking, letting Raya's images flow off her tongue.

They were jumbled. Memories, emotions, dreams.

"This job is important to her. Personally and professionally."

Images of Ian overwhelmed everything. It was confusing. Anger. Hurt. Love, such a deep love, it took Ana's breath away for a moment.

"We were right to keep Ian close to her."

Ana gasped. "She's been aboard some of those ships, Carson." She drew in a shaky breath. "We were lucky to get to those survivors before they got to the ship," she said, referring to the case they had worked which had led them to investigating Chuck's prison break.

"What are they being taken for?"

Ana shook her head. "I don't know. She doesn't know, either. They're not well cared for, at least not on board the ships, they aren't."

A young man's face loomed in her mind, pushing her heart up into her throat.

Raya's driving force. Whatever she was doing, this was driving her.

Her brother? Shocking red hair with freckles, and gray eyes the same as Raya's.

The image wavered between the young healthy memory to a later, older one; gaunt, pale, and so very unwell.

Ana pushed those memories aside and tried to find something related to the mob boss they were preparing to target.

Raya's feelings about the man were crystal clear. She abhorred him. She maintained the same controlled barrier in his presence as she'd tried to maintain when she'd been trapped with Ana and Ian in the cabin.

Ian had been a fissure in that wall. A fissure that had expanded enough to allow Ana access to glimpses of Raya's inner world.

And the true sense of desperation that was driving her to complete this job he'd hired her to do flawlessly.

She needed to get close to him.

She needed information from him.

She really is working for a higher purpose. Ashray the Mercenary was just a legend.

Raya was in for the long haul, going deeper into the underworld. The crime boss was a step to yet another knot in the network.

"Carson, I don't know if we can raid the compound. She's supposed to be going in long term."

"I know."

There was a hitch in Carson's voice that Ana almost missed. Her gaze shot to his face.

A maw opened in Ana's gut. She drew a deep breath, trying to separate Raya's memories and emotions from her own.

Whatever they did, it would affect Raya's ability to infiltrate the mob boss' network. Raya was working her way deeper and deeper for crucial intelligence. It was incredibly dangerous.

It really wasn't only about her personal quest to find her brother. She was fully committed to do what she had to.

"She could flip on us."

"I know that too. We're aware she'll do what she needs to do."

"Ian isn't going to like this."

"No. No, he won't," Carson said, suddenly looking very tired.

"Having them together gave me a chance to get in. This could lead to further complications later on."

"I'll deal with Ian when I have to."

"This mission, it's big, isn't it?" Lirikai asked, her voice solemn. "We will support her?"

"We just have to wait and see what happens. Be prepared for anything. I'm going to call Maeda to see if he can reach out to Teddy. We may need some help on this." Carson said, then grinned at Analiese. "Missing your cushy office?"

She smiled back, "I'm sure Freddy is keeping things warm for my return."

"Poor kid."

SEVENTEEN

"CARSON, I STILL DON'T like this," Ian said as he stepped up onto the dock, where he met with his old friend and his new colleagues.

"She has the tracker?"

Ian nodded. "Lirikai gave it to her. I have a feeling she isn't going to make this easy."

"They never do." Carson muttered. "It doesn't matter. We know she's going to Montreal to meet with Chuck's boss, so we'll be ready."

"It's still difficult to wrap my mind around how much she's changed."

"Everyone changes. That's life. Sometimes, to the outside world it's a sudden turnabout when the reality is that it was really a slow burn change. Looks to me like you're the slow burn type."

"Me?"

"Yeah. You've changed. Microscopically, I'll admit, but there are still changes."

Ian snorted.

"Well, you're here, aren't you? I figured it was an incredible shot in the dark that you'd haul your ass out of your lake to come and help us investigate this case. And look at you! You're practically a GPSA agent. *And* I didn't miss the fact you're letting go of your grudge against Maeda. You're almost a whole new man!"

"This guy thinks he's funny. And you've gotta put up with him every day?" Ian asked Analiese as he slid into the backseat next to her.

She was already belted in, hand gripping the support handle above the window. "You get used to it." She winked. She quickly adjusted her grip as Lirikai started the car. "I don't mind doing some of the driving, Lirikai. You must be tired." She prompted, hopeful.

"Don't you worry Ana, I'm just fine. I actually really enjoy driving."

"Damn." Ana muttered, sliding lower in her seat, then changed her mind, and sat upright again with a sigh.

The car swerved from its stopped position and they were on the highway in seconds, headed north.

Ian could hear Ana's teeth grinding.

"Keep an eye out for State patrol." Lirikai said to Carson.

"I am, don't worry there. Your speeding tickets are going to put us in the poor house, honey."

"What's a poor house?"

"Never mind."

Ian's mind drifted as they began chatting softly between themselves about Odson and something that was happening with a tribe of dragons off the east coast near Bermuda.

Glancing toward the window, he unhooked his hand from his own support bar, not having realized he'd reached for it.

He tried to relax and let his thoughts return to Raya.

The instant he'd touched her, it was like no time had passed between them.

What now?

They couldn't go back to the way things were before. He didn't know if there could even be a 'they' at all. Was it an option? Did he want it to be? Would she?

Raya had changed too much, but maybe not in the ways that really mattered.

He always knew she was strong. She had to be. That was never in question.

Now that he realized how selfish he'd been, he had a lot of work to do to make it up to her.

He sighed. The landscape whipped past.

The car's speed eased as they passed a parked state trooper. As soon as they crested a hill, Lirikai increased the speed again.

As much as he was wary of Lirikai's driving, he was fully aware that were he the one driving, he'd probably be flooring it all the way to Montreal.

Raya's new life—and Carson's job as a GPSA agent—was at an intersection that had Ian right in the middle. The reality of the situation was seeping into his bones, making them itch.

Ian had walked away from the human world so very long ago, when they'd run his family out of their territory with violence.

His family had maintained a long-standing friendship with the local Pictish tribe. His tattoos were a reminder of that alliance. Some visiting missionary had come along and labeled Ian's family 'Evil Monsters', causing the tribe to turn on them.

They'd left their lake, no longer wanted by their neighbors, and had elected not to slaughter the ignorant fools. Instead, they'd found other lakes to inhabit and learned to stay hidden. His mother had taken it hard. She'd loved her little humans.

Homesick, he had gone back from time to time, once the memory of his family had faded and locals no longer feared the monsters in the loch. Now, they capitalized on them.

For centuries, Ian held on to that experience from his youth. Right up until it affected his relationship with Raya. He'd been blind to the tension it caused in her. No that wasn't right. He wasn't blind. He'd willfully ignored it. Added to it.

And here she was. On her own, deep in the underbelly of not just the filthy human underworld, but that of the paranormal underworld too, it seemed.

Exploiters will exploit the vulnerable.

He glanced up at Carson and Lirikai, their voices a constant murmur of conversation.

Carson was created to protect the humans. Lirikai, as a Barra'kidai, sought vengeance on the exploitive. And Ana?

For them, it didn't seem to be an Us versus Them. Paranormal versus human.

Ian had to shed his old way of thinking. He hadn't even noticed when it stopped serving him.

In the past, he'd wanted Raya to live a sheltered life with him. Away from the pressures of her human mother's influence and the outside world.

He still wanted to protect her; he was driven to. He loved her too much to just step back and let her walk away again. Alone.

If she was going to walk in through the maw of the underground, he'd be there to split that gullet open if she needed an out.

They were going into a place where he might not be able to shift, to battle with his teeth and powerful size.

The last time he'd battled in his human form it was all swords and shields and fists and feet. And sometimes foreheads. That was fifteen centuries ago. He doubted Carson had a sword or a solid mace in his trunk.

He blew out a breath, catching sight of the disappearing mountain range out of the opposite window and noticed Ana's gaze locked on his face.

"What?"

"As GPSA agents, we carry guns when we need to." She smiled. "Your emotions are flooding the car."

"Think Carson will have a spare?"

"I do. I can share, if you know how to shoot?"

He chuckled. "Point the open end at the target and squeeze?"

"Carson, we should find a place to teach Ian how to shoot."

"Oooh, target practice!" Lirikai said, glancing at Ian in the rearview mirror.

"He isn't licensed."

"I won't tell if you won't." Ana said.

Carson turned and looked at Ana. "Seriously? Did *you* just say that?"

"Total self-preservation. I don't want to get shot in the ass if he happens to steal one from somewhere."

"Thanks for the vote of confidence, guys."

RAYA STOOD ON THE road between two tiny parked sedans, staring at the front of the townhouses, with a plastic bag from a nearby *Depanneur* clutched in her hands. The city was all shades of dawn-gray.

This was not the posh condo Chuck had talked up to his prison mates for the last few months. No wonder they hadn't figured out where he lived. It was low key and in the heart of the city.

This was an historic two-story building that she wished she had the keys to. Reaching into the bag, she withdrew the other half of the chocolate bar and stuffed it in her mouth as Chuck poked around the flowerpots. She'd reluctantly gone into the corner store after his fifth request for a jug of chocolate milk for his love. A little thing he always did for him when he came home.

"Whatever, just stay out of sight. And if you try to run, I will find you. You know this." She grumbled, then realized she was ravenous and bought an armload of junk food which she reluctantly shared with Chuck on the last block and half to his place. She'd kept her eye on him through the window while she was in the shop, in case he decided to make a run for it; she would have.

Chuck hadn't. Maybe his desperation had him gambling all-in on her soft heart or mercenary greed.

"Ha!"

A moment later, he stepped off the matchbook sized front garden with a key held aloft like a prize. Quickly scraping the mud from his shoes on the side of a neighboring stone wall, he bounced up the short flight of stairs.

The cross into Canada had been slow. She'd managed to guide Chuck safely along, much like she had during the prison break. She called LeVoleur when they reached tiny village of Carignan, Quebec, before abandoning the Richelieu River to go overland toward the St. Lawrence River.

Although LeVoleur was delighted they were both still alive, he reproached her tardiness in contacting him with her report.

He confirmed that he wanted her to retrieve an individual, vital to the health of his business. Now that she'd proved herself capable this far, they would discuss the retrieval fees on her arrival.

Fucker.

Raya swallowed the chocolate, casting a quick glance up and down the dimly lit street, and followed Chuck past the beautifully carved front door.

Chuck closed the door with a soft click as Raya squeezed into the narrow foyer alongside him. Even in the near-lightless space, she could see the glimmer in his eyes as he held his finger up to his lips and slipped out of his shoes. She did likewise and followed him toward the back of the house to the kitchen.

This really was not what she was expecting.

After weeks and weeks of planning, spying, waiting and walking—so much walking—this moment felt surreal. The misleadingly shabby cabin in the mountains had been weird. Standing in the homey kitchen of the man she broke out of prison for working with his crime boss uncle, running a human trafficking ring, felt more so.

She stared at the faded sticky notes on the fridge. They were all love notes, written in two distinct styles. She decided the cramped, messy notes were Chuck's. The elegant script of the other reminded her of the notes Dom used to leave in her room when he needed to her to swap out the laundry, or do some other favor for him.

She swallowed hard and drew a breath. Goddess, she missed him.

This was not the Chuck she'd shadowed in the prison or secretly observed at meetings with LeVoleur before making contact. This was someone else, living a completely different life.

Was she in the right place, or was he trying to screw her over too?

She stood in the middle of the kitchen, staring.

He opened the fridge, shoved the chocolate milk onto the top shelf, and grunted. "We're out of bread. Do you want anything?"

She blinked.

Who was this man?

"Washroom?"

He pointed his thumb to a door off the end of the kitchen.

She walked into the tiny powder room that held a cloud of apple cinnamon infused air.

Sitting on a toilet after several days of using bushes felt like a luxury, no matter how tiny the powder room was. As she washed her hands, she glanced around for the source of the fragrance and found a small plug-in. The scent reminded her of her childhood. Her father would often bake apple pie, heavy on the cinnamon. She inhaled the spicy sweet air, letting the tremor of longing ripple through her.

Raya stared at her reflection in the small ornate mirror above the sink. There were dark smudges under her eyes, and her shoulders drooped. This job had taken unexpected turns at every possible junction. The constant need to pivot was incredibly draining and she was still processing it all, mindful that the exhaustion could affect her judgement.

She dried her hands, then stepped back out into the kitchen.

"Chuck?" A man's uncertain voice pulled their attention.

Raya's gaze shot to the darkened entry. The dull morning light teasing the patio doors barely illuminated the figure standing in the doorway, clutching a hockey stick and staring at Chuck by the open fridge door.

Her heart stopped. "Dom?"

His head whipped in her direction and the stick clattered to the floor. "Oh my god, Ray? What the hell are you doing here? Either of you?" A second later the fridge door slammed shut and Chuck had his arms wrapped around Dominique.

She watched her brother kiss Chuck with intense longing and urgency.

She swallowed hard and turned her gaze to the view out on the back garden.

Her heart had finally kick-started again.

What. The. Fuck.

Chuck's lover was her brother.

Dom *is* alive.

Is this really happening? Or is this some kind of weird dream?

Maybe she was actually still in the forest, wandering in a haze of hallucinations.

Wave after wave of emotion threatened to bring her to her knees. Closing her eyes to stop the tears, she pressed a palm to the door frame as her world tilted. She sucked in a deep breath, feeding oxygen to her brain to process what was happening. She needed to get control over her shock. First Ian, now Dom.

She'd finally found him. Alive. And in those fleeting seconds, she could clearly see he was healthy. Everything she'd done since he'd gone missing was for this moment. To see his face for herself.

Everything had become so convoluted.

Think.

She was supposed to deliver Chuck's lover to the head of a powerful crime ring.

It was too much. And she didn't have time to break. Not now.

"Ray?" Dom's voice was soft at her side. Uncertain. Like when they were small and he stood in the door to her bedroom clutching a stuffed animal in the wee hours of the night after a bad dream. "I don't know why you're here, but I'm glad to see you. It's been a long time."

She turned to look up at her little brother. Relief warred with anger. "It has."

The uncertainty in his expression twisted her heart. The second her arms lifted a fraction, his were wrapped around her waist, his face buried in her shoulder. "I've missed you, Ray."

Her arms held his shoulders in a death grip, she was sure they'd both be bruised, they held each other so hard.

"So, this is weird." Chuck's voice snapped the tenor of the moment.

Raya opened her eyes, blinking away the tears. Beyond the glass of the patio door, the sun was finally cresting. A blazing ball of orange, suspended between the jagged horizon of the city-scape and the thick gray clouds blanketing the sky.

She stayed in the moment a little longer, allowing the sun to fill her vision and her heart, to welcome her brother's embrace.

He finally pulled away. The light of the rising sun illuminated his shock of copper hair and eyes, turning them from gray to smoky quartz. Like her own. Like their father's.

"We have a lot to talk about." She said.

"No shit." Chuck said. "Tea?"

Seriously. Who the fuck *was* this guy? "Yes, thanks."

EIGHTEEN

STANDING AROUND THE ISLAND counter with steam rising from teacups, Raya stared at her brother. The sun made its way above the layer of cloud. In the dull light from outside, she stared at her brother, really looking at him now.

There was no doubt he was healthy.

The last time she'd seen him—months before he disappeared—he'd been gaunt from addiction. He no longer looked skeletal, or had the deep bruising under his eyes. His skin was smooth and his hair had lost that stringy droop. It stood out in thick red waves.

"I see the resemblance, now that the two of you are side by side, but I'd have never guessed otherwise," Chuck said, looking from one to the other.

Dominique turned to Raya. "Okay, I saw on the news that Chuck had escaped prison-"

"So you're fully aware he's a convict?" Raya cut in.

"-but how do *you* figure into this? And yes." He said, chin rising a notch. "I am."

"You know what he's been convicted of?"

He nodded. "He doesn't do that anymore."

She stared in disbelief, eyes darting between the two. Chuck glared at her, mouth compressed.

This was wrecked.

She rolled her shoulders, took a generous swallow of tea, which scalded her tongue and throat, and decided to go right at it. She cleared her throat. "I'm here to collect and deliver you to Chuck's uncle. A crime boss. You know that too, right?"

Dom blanched. "I see." His gaze slid to Chuck.

"Nicki, she broke me out of prison to do this job. She's not going to finish it. Are you?" he challenged her. "You're going to take the money I offered and walk away."

"I'm so confused. Raya doesn't break anyone out of prison or have dealings with crime lords. And she never, ever does things for money. She's a peaceful, gentle soul."

Chuck erupted. His laughter bounced off the counter-top and kitchen cupboards. "Gentle. That's funny, Nicki. How come you never told me you had a sister? Or even better, a sister that is a shifter? Or that she's *the* fucking Ashray? That might have been helpful information, love."

"It never came up. How do you know about shifters? And what do you mean 'the' Ashray"

"Are you aware Chuck is a shifter too?"

Dom turned big eyes on Chuck "What? No. What are you?"

"He's a jellyfish." Raya couldn't suppress the smirk.

Chuck puffed up. "I'm a Man-O-War jellyfish."

"He's actually kind of pretty." She sipped her tea, glancing at her brother's open-mouthed expression.

"I don't know either of you," Dom said, staring from one to the other.

"Likewise," Raya said putting her cup down.

"What's that supposed to mean? I'm not the one with a title beginning with 'The', breaking people out of prison. Or revealing that I'm a shifter." This last accusation landed on Chuck.

"You-" Raya stopped at the elevated sharpness of her own voice, took a breath and resumed at a controlled volume. "The last time I saw you, Dominique, you were doped out and on the verge of death. Do you remember that? Do you remember the argument we had when I tried to help you? I bet you don't." She couldn't hold the raw emotion back any longer. "You went missing. They told us you were dead. Mom blamed me. She guilted me into finding you because I failed to protect you in the first place. Just like she blamed me for everything since Dad died."

"I-" Dominique's voice broke.

"No, Dom. You dropped off the face of the earth, you don't get to be righteous. I have spent all this time—*all* this time—doing everything I had to, in order to find you. Alive or dead."

"And now you're going to hand him over to my uncle." Chuck cut in.

"Right now, I'm fucking tempted, Chuck."

"So you're not?"

"I didn't say that."

Dominique and Chuck went so still her own breathing sounded like a roaring furnace in her ears. She took a controlled sip of her tea and placed it very deliberately back on the marble countertop.

Ian slid his foot forward as far as he could under the car's dashboard. They had been parked along the narrow street for a while, now. "How long are we going to sit here?" he asked Carson, as a black car with tinted windows rolled past theirs. They'd changed seating positions, with Carson behind the wheel and Ian upfront. Lirikai and Ana were curled up against their respective windows.

He yawned and reached for his third cup of coffee.

They'd spent the dark hours monitoring the waterways bordering the southern half of Montreal, looking for Raya and Chuck. Even though Carson had given her a tracker, he didn't trust she'd use it, and he wanted to know where she was.

She still hadn't activated it.

Just before dawn, they were spotted crossing the river to the island city, going straight inland to a quiet little street lined with century-old townhouses. He glanced at the ornate door she'd gone into for the hundredth time.

The black car slid past them again and pulled into the line of parked cars at the far end of the block. "Company?"

"Looks like." Carson grunted into his paper coffee cup. "This may get interesting."

"She can't shift after sunrise."

"I've seen her file. She'll be fine."

Ian had also experienced Raya's capabilities. The instinct to protect his mate lunged to the surface. The hand resting on his thigh began to tap.

"Patience."

The doors of the new car swung open and four figures rose up from it in the dim morning light.

His beast growled.

His hand hovered over his thigh as his breath lodged in his throat. "They shouldn't have been able to fit in that little car."

"It's Montreal, everyone drives small cars. They're used to it." Carson nodded to the cars parked in front of them.

Ian's right hand drifted toward the handle of his door.

"We don't want to complicate things."

"*We* don't?" He eyed the four large complications headed straight for the door Raya had disappeared through.

"Watch and wait."

"Dog's bollocks."

"Yup, this sucks." Carson took another sip.

NINETEEN

RAYA JUST NEEDED THIRTY seconds to think things through.

LeVoleur was expecting her to deliver Chuck and his lover. Obviously, something to do with witnessing operations. What else could it be? Why now, after all these years?

She'd let Chuck believe he could buy her off in order to get his cooperation. He didn't know the real reason behind the work she was doing. All of it was to find her brother Dominique.

Correction. It *had* been all about finding Dominique. It had become much more complicated since she'd been enlisted by the *Organization* to help break the ring. There were still so many others out there being sold into human trafficking. That hadn't stopped—and wouldn't.

She couldn't walk away now, as tempting as it was.

Ian's image rolled through her brain so hard it brought with it the memory of his scent and touch. She sucked in a breath.

We're not finished yet.

Could she walk away from Chuck and Dom? Let them live in peace while she found another way to do the job she'd taken on?

Chuck was a convicted human trafficker—and Dominique knew about it!

She groaned.

So fucked up.

Her gaze lingered on her brother's face, drinking in the sight of him. For so very long she'd waited for this moment.

"How did the two of you meet?" she asked him.

"I told you. Nicki and I met at the beach." Chuck said.

"So you did." She turned to her brother. "I want to know how you ended up with a guy that deals in human merchandise, Dom."

Color flooded Dom's face. "I uhm...I was living with some friends in the party district, close to the beach where the tourists kept things lively. Every week there were new faces to hang out and have a good time with." His eyes dropped to his hands.

Her gut tightened and her heart twisted. She knew what that meant. She reached out and slid her hand over his.

"This particular week, Chuck walked into the club with a bunch of guys. I approached him. And we just..." He shrugged. "We just hit it off. We met up each night. He was different from the other guys I'd met."

She thought of Ian. She'd never met anyone else like him. They just clicked when they met. Still did.

This was different. Ian didn't work for a crime boss stealing people from vacation havens. Chuck was nothing like Ian.

Dominique drank some of his tea. "His buddies insisted on having a big end of vacation bash one Saturday night before going back to wherever they were from. The partying was more intense than the previous nights, of course."

"Of course," she said, voice flat.

"I went into the bathroom to take another hit from the stash one of the guys had. Then I went looking for Chuck. I ran into his buddies instead. I'm not sure what happened. It was a bad hit. I woke up in a cold, dark room in nothing but my underwear. I wasn't alone; there were others. We were in a steel box."

Raya knew exactly what he was talking about. She'd been on two ships with humans imprisoned in steel cargo containers. She squeezed his hand. "How did you get out?"

Dominique lifted his gaze to his lover. "Chuck. He got me out the night the boat was supposed to leave. I've never been so scared in my life."

"I couldn't just leave him there." Chuck said, his voice catching in his throat.

"What about all the others?"

He looked away, toward the back garden and shrugged. When he turned back to her, he wore a deep scowl. "It's not like I ever wanted to be part of that. When you work for my uncle, you do what you're told."

"You could have worked for someone else? You know, got a real job." She snapped.

"It was quick and easy money to begin with. Little things here and there. The more respect you earn, the more important the job. The more he trusts you. And that trust is powerful. And before you know it, you're doing all kinds of stuff you never would have imagined."

"So, you worked for your uncle stealing people for profit, so you could feel good about pleasing him."

"He did. That all stopped after we got together."

"Did it? Then how was Chuck caught on a ship full of kidnap victims on the west coast, which landed him in prison, Dom?"

"He didn't have a choice. He pushed for Chuck to do the job, even after he told him he wasn't doing it anymore."

"Right. Nothing to do with money, maybe? This is a nice place."

"Who the fuck are you to judge me? You're a fucking mercenary, for Christ's sake. You get paid to hunt people down." He turned to Dominique. "I offered to pay her off."

Dom snatched his hand away from Raya's.

She straightened. "It isn't nearly what your uncle is paying me."

Chuck's mouth dropped open, his eyes sliding to Dom. "You wouldn't. You wouldn't turn him over. Not now."

"What did you call me, Chuck? *The* Ashray? I'm a mercenary with a reputation that your uncle paid for. A reputation of getting things done. I'm hired for a job. I do it. Simple. I've come a long, long way from the person you used to know, little brother."

Should she tell them that she wasn't really a mercenary? That it was all a front to find him? To get the information she needed to break the network? Could she find another way to get that information, without handing him over to the crime lord?

She doubted LeVoleur would let her anywhere near him if she failed this job. Infiltration would be so much easier. Easier access to his inner circle, gleaning bits of information that might not be kept on a computer, phone or some other physical database. Some things just weren't committed to paper or digital files.

So far, all of her jobs were confined to the crime world. Criminal on criminal work. This was the first time she was having to deal with an innocent.

She studied Dominique's face then let her gaze slide to Chuck.

Could Chuck have that information? Being so close to the boss, he must know things and people. She'd spied him at the few key meetings she'd been able to infiltrate. Did LeVoleur trust Chuck to keep his mouth shut? Were she a crime boss, she wouldn't trust Chuck. Or was he as much at risk as Dom was, now that LeVoleur knew Chuck had stolen his merchandise from him and set up house?

Raya didn't trust him.

"Chuck, why does your uncle want Dom? And why now?"

"He was on the ship, he saw faces."

"Who did you see, Dom?"

"I don't know who they were. While we were being held, a large group of businessmen came in. It looked like some sort of tour. They all had different accents and some spoke in other languages."

"They must have been very important, Chuck. Who were they?" she said turning her full attention back to him.

"Why?" His eyes had turned assessing. He was trying to guess the motive behind her line of questioning.

The identity of those men might be the key to breaking the network. The crime boss wanted Dom because he was the one victim that had escaped, *and* had seen the faces of important men. Those men likely needed to keep their identities safe from public knowledge of their clandestine activities.

She looked from Chuck to Dom. They were on borrowed time.

Raya had to somehow get Dom to the GPSA, then to her contacts with the *Organization*.

"Your uncle is expecting my call."

Chuck glared at her with murder in his eyes from across the countertop.

He slid sideways around the counter and lunged at her.

Raya sidestepped, locked her hand on his throat and used his unbalanced momentum to pin him to the tiled floor.

He groaned from the impact.

"Second strike, Chuck. Third, and you're out. Understand?"

She glanced up at her wide-eyed brother, then let go of Chuck's throat.

Chuck gasped for air and scrambled to his feet.

"Do you understand?"

He nodded, backing toward Dominique.

She reached into her pocket for the burner phone from the last backpack she'd planted. Her fingers grazed the tracker Lirikai had given her from Carson.

"I'm going to step out into the back garden to think."

The tension in Chuck's expression eased. Hope.

She went to the front door to retrieve her discarded boots. On her way back, she brushed her hand along her brother's shoulders which made him start. "I just need a few minutes. Don't get any more brilliant ideas, Chuck." She slipped into her boots and slid the patio door open. She stepped out, inhaling the fresh air.

With a final glance at her brother through the open door, she strode across the small deck and down to the flagstones, hands in her pockets.

What the fuck do I do?

She couldn't deliver Dominique to the crime lord. He'd kill him.

She needed to get him to a safe place. He'd been safe here for a long time. Could she just leave him here while she made other arrangements?

How long could she hold off on calling LeVoleur before he became suspicious? She'd contacted him at the last cache point, so he was expecting to hear from her by midday.

The flowers lining the path pulled her attention.

She crouched down to look at the beautiful healthy petals while she laced her boots. Fragile. Vibrant. Healthy. Like her brother finally was.

She inhaled deeply of the fragrance that infused the early morning air.

Priceless.

She smiled as a bee landed on lily and got to work. The work this little guy did would ripple out, helping other plants to thrive.

She stood and turned to head back inside. She could hear Chuck and Dom's low voices cut by the ringing of the doorbell.

"Are you expecting company?" she asked Dominique.

"No. No one ever comes here, especially at this hour, and it's Sunday, so no deliveries, either." They both looked alarmed.

"Get your shoes." She said.

"Good idea," a voice said as a figure moved to block the open patio door. "Nice place, Chuck."

"Fuck." Chuck gasped.

"Francois," Raya said, recognizing the man as one of LeVoleur's enforcers. "Boss is impatient, is he?" How the hell had she not heard him come over the fence?

Francois shrugged. "He wanted us to make sure you had a ride. Thought you could use it after all that walking, or swimming, or whatever it is that you did."

"Thoughtful," Raya said, as she considered options. His bulk filled the doorway. She could take him down. Beyond him a second figure lingered in the back yard.

"He is, isn't he?" Francois grinned. "Chuck, be polite and open your front door for our friends."

Chuck, she knew, was exhausted after their long journey from the prison. How far could they run, if they needed, once she took down the two guys in the back yard? How long before the goons at the front door either forced it open or came around the back as well?

These guys wouldn't kill Chuck or Dominique. The boss wanted to see them first. She still had time to figure something out. She reached into her pocket as she reached for the last of her tea.

"Don't want be wasteful." She said as she slipped the tracker into the pocket of her brother's lounge pants while he stared at the neckless man in his kitchen. "Get your shoes; time to go," she said, as though rounding up a couple of wayward children.

"Chuck?" Dom's voice was strained.

"You're a heartless bitch." Chuck growled at Raya. "You're condemning your own brother."

"Brother, huh?" Francois smirked as he loomed next to Chuck, eying Raya and Dominique with curiosity.

Raya looked at her brother. Her heart twisted as her mask fell back into place. "The brother I knew died years ago," she said, loud enough for Francois to hear.

Dominique jerked as though she'd backhanded him, but he didn't say a word.

She resisted the urge to say anything more. To ease the sting of her words.

She couldn't risk it.

If—*if*—she could get him out of this alive, he would understand.

For now, she had to buy enough time to figure out just how to do that.

TWENTY

IAN'S BODY WAS STRUNG. He couldn't relax with those guys lurking on the front step to the house Raya was trapped in. The other two guys had disappeared up the street, most likely looking for a way around the back of the solid row of townhouses.

Minutes later the front door opened, and the two thugs stepped aside to make room for Raya to emerge from between them.

"Here we go," Carson muttered, as the sound of another vehicle approaching pulled Ian's focus from Raya.

A black SUV pulled alongside their car and rolled to a stop across from the open townhouse door.

Raya descended the stairs and two more figures emerged from the house. He recognized the first one as being the inmate from the prison. Then the second one came into view, followed by the two guys that had gone around the block.

"Holy fuck." Ian said, hand reaching for the door handle again as his gaze whipped back to Raya. "That's Ray's brother."

"Don't." Carson's voice stopped him. "Ana-"

"Yes, she turned the tracker on. It's active."

"This should be fun." Lirikai said, the glee evident in her voice.

"There are probably two more guys in that SUV." Carson murmured. "Ana-"

"Yes, Carson, I'm already texting Jack."

Ian turned to look at Analiese as she bent over her phone, her thumbs flying. She glanced up at him with a grin. "Long work relationship."

"I should be driving." Lirikai said, her hand on Carson's shoulder.

"No time for that," Ana said, before Carson could answer her.

As soon as everyone was piled into the two black vehicles, Carson started the car. He waited for them to turn the corner, then pulled away from the curb in pursuit.

"AH, THERE YOU ARE!" Jean-Guy LeVoleur beamed as Raya stepped off the elevator. "I knew I made a good decision when I hired you. Phenomenal."

She tipped her head forward, "Mr. LeVoleur."

He guided them toward the penthouse suite with an adjoining boardroom. "I much prefer my home and offices in Quebec City, but this is serviceable. Would you like to sit?" he swept a hand toward a nearby leather couch.

"Thank you." She said, settling herself into a laid-back posture, creating the illusion of complete ease. Internally, there was a boulder settling in her chest. "It was very considerate of you to have the cars sent for us."

LeVoleur nodded, pleased by her acknowledgment. "After your last message, I had men watching for your approach. I thought you might be tired after your journey, and I was eager to be reunited with my wayward nephew, Charles," he said, finally turning to look at Chuck.

"Uncle." His voice was tight, his body rigid. Dominique stood next to him.

LeVoleur moved to stand before Dom. He studied him for a long moment, then turned away with a grunt and went back to Chuck. "You've put me in a difficult position, Charles. A dangerous position on one hand, and an exceedingly uncomfortable position on the other. I hate being at odds with your mother; she knows how to make my life miserable."

"What will you do with him?" Chuck asked, his attention glued to his uncle's face.

LeVoleur's thick brows rose. "You care for him that much, do you?"

"I do."

The boulder in Raya's chest grew a little bigger as she looked from Chuck to her brother, side by side, straight and tall, heads up and eyes forward.

He, too, had grown stronger in the last years. He'd always been physically strong, until the addiction took over. That was clearly in his distant past.

If he was afraid, he didn't show it.

She was proud of him in that moment.

As much as she really disliked Chuck, she grudgingly admitted to herself that, despite everything else, he'd been good for Dominique. They'd made a life together. A home. Until Chuck had gotten himself caught and incarcerated. Dom had stayed and waited for him.

She thought of Ian.

Would they have had such a life, had things been different?

They had for a time.

Until this man's operations upended her world. Not just hers. Many, many others, too.

Her meeting with LeVoleur would end shortly, and she would be expected to depart, now that her job had been completed.

What would become of Chuck and Dom, if she walked away now? He'd made his decisions with eyes wide open.

Her mother's voice slid up the back of her spine.

Protect your little brother. He's your responsibility. He's just a helpless human.

Ian's face loomed in her mind. He didn't have room in his life for humans. And he hated the unbearable sense of responsibility her mother had dumped on her shoulders all her life. It was the main reason he'd been unable to get along with her.

She hoped the tracker she placed in Dom's pocket was functional, and Ian's GPSA friends were on their game.

LeVoleur paced the room. Everyone else stood waiting, silent. Two guards stood by the main door, another two lingered by the edges of the room. To stop their escape? Or something more?

"You betrayed my trust, Charles," LeVoleur finally said. "You know how I feel about trust. It's very important to me. You also know what happens to those that betray me."

Chuck nodded. His Adam's apple worked up and down his throat several times.

"I'll deal with that situation later. Right now, I want to discuss business," he said, dismissing Chuck as he turned toward Raya.

She stood and followed him into the board room. Two of his guards slipped through the door and closed it behind them before taking up posts at either side of the room.

"Marie-Ange, call the others. Confirm the meeting time." LeVoleur spoke to a woman who'd been in the board room. At his command, she nodded and left the room.

Moving further into the room, Raya went to the window with a magnificent view of the city. The river was a glimmering ribbon behind the skyscrapers and heritage buildings.

She waited for LeVoleur to join her before she spoke softly so that his men would not hear. "Human retrieval fees are much higher than object retrieval."

"I'm aware."

She turned to look at him.

"You needn't scowl at me, Mademoiselle. I have no intention of fleecing you. I merely wanted to see how you handled the situation."

The entire break out and trek through the mountains had been a test.

"To what end?" she demanded.

"To ensure you lived up to the whispers. You are quite capable." He nodded.

"I know I am." She held his gaze, unflinching, waiting for him to elaborate.

"I'm proposing another job."

"You haven't paid me for the first one yet."

The money he owed her was substantial. She could use it to help Dominique find a new life.

He smiled. "That will be taken care of within the hour. I have something very specific I want you to do. Something *only* you can do. A special job. I want you to see the site."

She was aware of the door opening and the gentle clink of glasses that drew her attention to the back of the room. She jerked her head back to the view out the window.

Her heart stopped and the blood coursing through her body flooded her veins. She missed part of what LeVoleur had said.

TWENTY-ONE

WITH A FINAL RUNDOWN on the plan, the group split up and entered the towering hotel through different entrances.

Ian followed Ana to the elevators while Carson moved toward the long line at the check in counter. Lirikai disappeared down another hall entirely.

"From the tracker, I can't tell exactly what floor she's on, just the general area of the building. I'd bet my grandmother's poker luck they'll be on the top floor; mob bosses tend to enjoy luxury. The hotel schematics map out the penthouse suites." She punched the button for the fourteenth floor. "Quick stop to the housekeeping supply closet first."

Ian ignored the distinct feeling of the walls closing in during the trip up and focused on controlling his breathing.

As they stepped off the elevator, Ana fired off a text on her phone. "Lirikai is on her way."

She found a spare custodian jacket and housekeeping smock. With a quick glance down the hall, she wheeled the cart out of the closet and headed for the elevator. The doors opened and Lirikai handed them both gold key cards. The doors closed and Ana pushed the button for the second elevator car to take them up.

"I hope there isn't already a chambermaid working on their floor." The doors opened and Ana swiped her card, then jabbed the button for the penthouse.

Ana grabbed an ice bucket from her cart and shoved it into Ian's hands then pushed the linen trolley to the left and knocked on the first door. "Housekeeping."

Ian went right. Two of the guards that escorted Raya out of the townhouse that morning stood at the end of the hall just outside the double doors. He made a quick turn down the short vending and ice machine hall. There was another door marked employees. Using the card Lirikai had given him, he peeked inside and found another cart with glasses and water pitchers. There was a laminated map of the floor taped to the wall which told him exactly what each room was. He quickly filled the bucket and pitchers with ice and water and backed out of the tiny room.

The guards moved to block his progress as he reached the double doors.

"Refreshments for the board room, sirs."

"Don't disturb them." He opened the door to allow him through.

Ian nodded as he silently pushed the cart into the room and moved toward the corner where he set down the clean glasses and sweating pitcher. As he gathered the used glasses to the lower shelf of the cart, he glanced around.

His heart jumped when his eyes met Raya's. They widened in surprise before she dropped her gaze and turned away.

She was listening to a stout man in a tailored suit talk, as he faced the panorama of the city outside the window.

Ian guessed that was LeVoleur. Two more guards stood to either side of the room. One stared ahead, the other monitored Ian's movements.

Ian nodded respectfully to the guard, then proceeded to poor fresh glasses of ice water to be placed on the sideboard.

"I would be very interested in a tour of the site before I decide to accept the contract." Raya said to the man. "I'll let you know in a couple of days after I've had a chance to rest and consider."

"I'm afraid a couple of days from now would be too late. I have arranged a room for you just down the hall. Go and rest and refresh yourself. I'll take you for that tour later this evening," he said, turning away from the window to face Raya.

She appeared to consider this for a moment, then nodded. "I wouldn't want to impede your schedule. Tonight is acceptable."

He nodded. "Francois will walk you out."

Ian was about to push the cart through the open door after Raya and Francois when the mob boss' voice stopped him. "You."

He froze midway through the door. Had he given himself away?

He turned to see the man with an arm raised and finger extended toward him. "Water."

Ian rested the open door against the cart so he could walk over to the sideboard to retrieve a fresh glass of ice water. Approaching the mob boss he held it out to him.

The man stared hard at him.

Dread settled in his gut. Had he blown it already? Had he put Raya at risk? He couldn't be sure.

His heart pounded, more thoughts racing through his head as the man stared at him another moment before reaching for the glass.

"You move very quietly for such a large man. You do your job well." His eyes swept the neat rows of glasses at the back of the room. "I'm always looking for men like you to join my team. Little jobs. Easy jobs. Someone who takes pride in his job." He pulled a business card from a pocket inside his jacket and held it out for Ian. "If you'd like a job that pays more call that number."

"Thank you, sir."

Ian took the card and made his exit. By the time he reached the hall, Raya and Francois were nowhere in sight. Ana's cart was parked at the far end of the hall. He acknowledged the two guards who still stood outside the board room doors, and continued pushing the cart back to the short hall where the employee room was, and left it as he found it. Glancing around at some of the open boxes of supplies, he grabbed an arm load of linens and toiletries and headed toward the parked supply cart, fully aware of the guards' attention on his movements.

As he was placing the supplies on the cart, Ana emerged from a room. Seeing what he was doing she smiled and said in a voice that carried "Awe, you are so kind to do that for me."

"Anything for a pretty lady such as yourself." He said, hand to heart. "Will you join me at break time?"

She glanced at her watch, "I'm nearly finished. Would you mind taking these to that room right there?" She asked, grabbing some of the soaps and towels. "And I'll join you shortly?"

"Of course."

With the supplies in hand he gave the door a light rap. When it opened, Raya stood in the doorway. "I'll just put these in place for you."

She stepped aside for him to enter then let the door close.

"I'm alone."

He shoved the towels and bottles on the bathroom counter just inside the door then pulled her into his arms and held tight.

She stood rigid at first then relaxed after a moment.

"Ian," her voice was soft. "Dominique. Dominique was in that house, he's what I was meant to retrieve for LeVoleur."

"I saw him."

Her mask slipped so that her lovely face was a mixture of heartfelt relief and terror. "Goddess, I can't believe I found him, here of all places! With Chuck, of all people! He's in trouble, real trouble."

"We have to get you out of here."

"I'll be fine. I know what I'm doing. The tracker is in Dom's pocket. I don't think he noticed I slipped it in. I need you to promise me you'll protect him. No matter what."

"If things do go sideways and it comes down to you or him, you know I'll always protect-"

"Him, Ian. I need you to protect *him*."

He was about to shake his head.

"Promise me. I can't lose him again. Promise me."

It was the last thing he wanted to do. The look in her eye and the strength of her resolve twisted his heart. "I'll do what I can."

She searched his face, wanting something more. She finally nodded.

His thumb traced the edge of her plump lower lip. "I still..."

She bounced up onto the tip of her toes and locked her lips to his. His arms instantly enveloped her, crushing her to him. The taste of her sweet mouth reminded him how much he loved her. How much he wanted her to be in his arms for the rest of their lives.

She had an important job to do, and he was going to do everything he could to ensure she succeeded.

She suckled his lip, then released it with a sigh and pressed her forehead to his jaw.

He could feel the words between them, though she maintained her silence.

"I have to go."

She nodded and stepped back.

It took everything he had in him not to pull her back to him again.

His eyes held hers a moment longer before he turned away and joined Ana in the hall by the elevator.

"All set?" she asked, voice light and bright as she pushed her cart toward the opening doors of the elevator.

"All set." He smiled.

RAYA CLOSED HER EYES when the door clicked shut after Ian.

She had a job to do.

As much as she appeared confident on the outside, her stomach was a knot of worry.

Another job offer.

It was what she wanted. To get closer. Go deeper. Get to the heart of the network.

Yet Dom's life was on the line.

If he were anyone else, how would she approach the situation?

She didn't like collateral damage. Still, she needed that distance. And she wasn't sure how she could achieve that.

She walked to the window that looked out over the city of Montreal. The reality of Dom's presence in this situation had started to settle into her while they were still at his house. Now that she stood here alone, it overwhelmed her in waves.

Ian was here. Another potential point of danger. During their time together, the years had been peaceful and quiet. He'd told her tales of battles in the old days. She knew he could fight if needed, though in a world of semi-automatic guns? She wasn't so sure.

Turning away from the window, she lay down on the bed and closed her eyes. She had to wait for nightfall.

The tears came.

She'd done it. She'd found Dominique and he was alive.

For now. Her mother's voice rose up from the back of her mind.

But alive. She insisted.

She gave into the blackness of exhaustion.

Her eyes popped open. The room was illuminated by the city lights, the sky differing shades of charcoal and indigo.

Dominique.

Reaching for the pull of the water she could sense running through the pipes and underground streams, far below her, deep under the surface of the city streets.

It fueled her essence.

The scent of living water filled her nose as she inhaled deeply and let her particles disperse, becoming part of the moisture in the air, and began to drift. Finding what crevices she could, she moved throughout the hotel floor. Through vents, around electrical outlets, out and in through open windows and doors, by-passing LeVoleur's men, Chuck, and Jean-Guy himself enjoying the company of some women in a scene she'd later need to scrub from her brain, until she found her brother in a room identical to the one she'd just left.

He was alone.

She materialized beside him by the window.

He jumped.

"You know it's always freaked me out when you did that. I never know where you're coming from." He turned toward her. "Did you see Chuck?"

She nodded. "He's fine. Pacing."

"Worried." He sighed, shoulders dropping. "He's been worried about this since he helped me escape."

She watched him. Gauging. Trying to come to a decision. Up until now, it seemed as though every other decision had been clear. Do or don't.

"Dom, what did you expect your future would be like, living with someone like him?"

"We were trying to bide our time until we could find a quiet way out."

"I don't know if that's possible. The work he's involved in-"

"Was. Was involved in. He was caught on the west coast because he had no choice in the matter. He never wanted to do the work."

"There is always a choice."

He straightened, staring down into her face.

He couldn't argue that. "People change."

"They do. What about the destruction left behind in their wake until they reach that lofty realization?"

"Who-the-fuck-are *you* to say that to *me*? You're a fucking mercenary. No better than *any* of them. At least Chuck was trying to get out. You're sinking your teeth as deep as you can."

She wanted to tell him.

If she did, how badly could it go if he told Chuck and Chuck tried to use it to get out of what he had coming?

"He could make amends."

Dom stared at her.

"He could work with the authorities to stop more people, like you, from being abducted and sold. To track and find the ones that have been trapped for years."

"Chuck? You want Chuck to make amends. What about you, you fucking hypocrite?" His voice was venomous.

She didn't flinch.

"Mom made it my life's responsibility to protect you, Dominique. Because I had the ability to do things you couldn't. From the time she realized you were human, she *made* me your guardian. She couldn't bear the thought of losing you after dad died."

"Dad's death wasn't your fault."

"I was there, Dom. When the accident happened; I couldn't help him."

"You were young. It wasn't your fault. I know what mom is like."

"Was."

He froze for a solid minute. "She's dead."

Raya nodded.

He let out a shuddery breath, rubbing a hand over his face.

"She gave in to her oblivion."

His eyes filled with tears.

She squared her shoulders. "Dom, they told us you drowned at that beach. By accident or suicide. They expected you were probably dead, with nothing further to be done. She demanded I search for you, but I had to know, too. I couldn't spend the rest of my life not knowing, Dom."

He looked up at her.

"That's all I've been trying to do since that day. Find you. Dead or alive. Just find you. And I have."

"Ray, I'm not your responsibility. Never was. That's why I left. I had to get away from this...drama between you and mom." The tears spilled down his cheeks.

"You *know* me, Dominique."

He faced her. Studying her now, after so long apart, his eyes searched hers.

She watched as he began to make the connections, his expression changing from anger to wonder. He blew out a breath.

He opened his mouth. Then closed it to try again. "You've always looked out for me. It's really not about the money."

She shook her head. She finally let her hand reach for him. "It never was."

He understood.

"What do I do?" he asked her.

"Trust me."

He nodded, sniffling.

"You can't tell Chuck. Not yet." She said quickly when he raised his head to look at her again. "Not *yet*."

She reached for his hand, squeezing it, then looked out the window.

"Please." Her voice pleaded with him. "I wasn't expecting to find you like this. I have to find a way to get you back into a safe place and finish the other things I have to do."

He turned to the window and pointed to a street to their right. "That's my house. I've been happy there."

"If I hadn't found you, someone else would have. LeV-oleur would have made sure of it. You have to realize that that sanctuary was always temporary. Help me find you a permanent one."

He straightened his shoulders, eyes clearing. Drawing in a breath he asked, "What do I do?"

"I just need you to trust me, no matter what happens. Stay close to Chuck if you can. I can see how much he loves you and will do what he has to, to keep you safe. And do not let on that anything has changed. I was never here."

He nodded. "Ray, I'll do whatever is needed to protect him, too."

"I will get you out. But I need to go in deeper."

Something flickered in his eyes. She thought it might be pride. She couldn't be sure.

"The Ashray, huh?" he grinned.

"I had to woman-up and get shit done."

He chuckled and pulled her into his arms. "I love you, Ray. I've missed you."

"I've missed you, too." She couldn't hide the emotion in her voice as she wrapped her arms around her little brother's waist. "I have to get back to my room."

She hesitated. "Nicki, huh?"

He grinned. "That's what Chuck likes to call me and I needed a new name anyway. You can still call me Dom."

"You're sure?"

He nodded and kissed her forehead. "Be safe."

"You, too."

His eyes followed her as she dissipated and drifted away.

Rematerializing in the room assigned to her, she went into the bathroom to wash her face and collect her thoughts and emotions.

Staring at her reflection in the mirror, she reviewed the sequence of events, trying to find the underlying pattern.

Was she in over her head?

She was so close to the next step down into the network.

Another league below the surface.

LeVoleur wasn't the heart of the network, but he was close to it.

How do I get Dom to safety without blowing my cover?

Ian was here. The GPSA agents probably were too.

She wasn't alone.

Her eyes closed and she swallowed hard.

I'm not alone.

I'm not alone.

I'm. Not. Alone.

She drew in a shaky breath.

There was a knock on her door.

Time to go.

TWENTY-TWO

THEIR SUV ROLLED UP to the security gate at the Port of Montreal, where the driver showed the guard some sort of paperwork. Night was fully settled and Raya could feel the pull of the river. It whispered to her magic, full of life and power.

The water always called to her at night. Like most nights lately, she had work to do, so she ignored it.

LeVoleur had offered her a new job. This was her chance to get the information she needed, and hopefully save her brother while doing it.

She'd taken a big risk—an incredibly big risk—trusting Dom. She hadn't trusted anyone in years. And she was hinging it all on her gut trust in Ian, that he'd pull through with agent Perenga and provide help if she needed it, or stay out of her way.

Above all, she needed two things. Her brother alive and free, and key information about the network.

She didn't know what the job was that LeVoleur wanted her to do. It seemed that her apparently ruthless loyalty to her personal mercenary code made him believe he could trust her to get things done.

She'd worked so hard to build that legend and now it was paying off.

She may have destroyed parts of her soul in the process, but she made her peace with her creator on a nightly basis. If there was an afterlife, she truly didn't know what lay in store for her. So long as she was able to save her brother and do her true work, she was okay with whatever she had to face.

The driver continued on, steering them past port workers, along rows of stacked shipping containers in faded dirty colors of rust, dust-bowl gold, and silt-smudged blue. Above them, the lights of a bulk carrier lit the port, bow pointed east toward the Atlantic Ocean.

She'd wondered.

All previous known trails were coastal, remaining far outside the interior and in the safety of open international waters.

If this was what she thought it was...this was bold.

"I'm expanding my business ventures." LeVoleur leaned toward her with a grin.

Were the men Dominique had seen on that other ship, all those years ago, investors?

"What does this have to do with the job you're proposing? I'm not a sailor."

"You, my dear, are a ghost. I need a ghost to ensure the quality of my employees."

She raised a brow as she looked at him.

"You have proven your reputation. You keep your contracts no matter what. My nephew made my operations look weakened. I don't know if there are others that might feel they can do as they wish with my merchandise as well. I suppose you can say I'm feeling a little vulnerable. And with Charles being my sister's son, I'm reluctant to make a true example of him. You see the difficulty he's put me in?"

"Hmm, I do." She paused as though considering. "However, I tend not to limit myself to one long term employer. You want to hire me, full time, to spy on your employees? I'm expensive."

"Free agent. I know. I'm sure we can agree on terms favorable to both of us."

"I will have to give this offer some deep consideration. I've always enjoyed my choice of jobs. I've never come under any one employer's payroll. I don't like being tied down."

The car passed a crane and rolled to a stop not far from an access bridge to the ship.

"Shall we go for a tour?"

IAN WATCHED OUT THE windshield as Lirikai guided the rental along Notre Dame Street at a safe distance behind the mob boss' SUVs.

Analiese was monitoring the tracker and watching the map on her phone. "We're coming up to the Port of Montreal."

Lirikai pulled the car over when the SUVs turned onto a service road toward the river. They could see the fencing and security gates from their stopped position.

"There's a public park just beyond here." Analiese said, moving the map across her screen.

"Good. We can park and approach from that side. They're probably headed for that ship." Carson said. "Avoid security cameras where possible. It's easier to manage post-op clean up if we don't have to confiscate footage, especially if anyone shifts. Once that stuff gets out, it's hard to get it back under wraps."

Ian nodded. "I've spent most of my life staying hidden from humans."

Carson snorted, "You're spotted all the time."

"Only when I get bored and want to mess with the tourists. Freaks them out, and it's amusing to see them scramble."

"Lirikai, slow down and take the next right." Analiese said. "Keep right. According to the satellite view, there's a park storage lot butted up against the port property."

"With those flood lights everywhere, it's going to be hard to get around unseen. If we can't find a way through or around the fence, go along the river." Carson said.

"I'll get the waterproof bags from the trunk." Analiese said, getting out of the car once it was stopped. She handed one to each of them as they approached the back of the car to grab any other gear they may need. She reached into her duffle bag and withdrew a holstered gun, checked it over, then handed it to Ian. "Remember-"

"Aye, I know. Safety off, point at the bad guy."

Ana handed them each an earpiece.

"Spread out, stay out of sight, avoid cameras. And keep an eye out for crew on that ship. We don't know if they're armed and looking for trouble. We have to assume there may be shifters among them," Carson ordered.

"I scented shifters at the hotel property. There may be some here," Lirikai said.

"You good, old friend?" Carson cast a look of concern toward Ian.

"It's been a long time since I've gone into battle. I'm not sure about this thing." He held up the holstered gun.

Carson shrugged and inserted the earpiece Ana had given him, nodding toward Ian to do the same. "They can be a useful deterrent."

"I also miss the old days of swords and sharp teeth," Lirikai said with a grin, and darted off into the shadows.

Ian followed Carson along the fence toward the river. "Ana, do you copy?"

"Copy."

"If you can't find a way through the fence, stay with the car in case we need a quick and direct escape."

"Copy that."

They crouched in the shadow of some bushes close to the river's edge. Carson's eyes were trained on the illuminated ship. It was the only one currently docked at the port. Through the foliage, they could see the two SUVs. Raya looked small surrounded by the mob members.

The instinct to protect her rose up hard in him.

"Stop snarling." Carson snapped.

"I'm going down to the river."

"Don't engage, she needs time to do her job."

"If she's in trouble-"

"Then we all have her back, Ian."

He nodded and made his way toward the water.

TWENTY-THREE

LEVOLEUR LED RAYA UP the short ramp to the ship's deck. Workmen were busy checking over their stations, with random thugs occupying spaces nearby, watching her and their boss.

They went up to the brightly lit bridge, where the pilots navigated the ship across oceans and lakes and along treacherous river routes like the St. Lawrence.

On seeing their approach, the ship's pilots backed away from the table where they were in deep discussion, and turned weary faces to LeVoleur and his guest. More thugs occupied the far corner of the space.

"Gentlemen, this is a new employee of mine, we're just giving her a tour of the place before she joins you as the new head of security."

The Captain's brows went up, looking from Raya to LeVoleur to the man standing guard in the corner.

Raya smiled at LeVoleur. "I haven't yet accepted your offer." She said, walking toward the large windows overlooking the ship's deck. From this height, she could see the guards posted across the deck and on the ground around the port surrounding any access to the ship. The bow was pointed toward the Atlantic and floodlights glittered off the water's black surface. Beyond the port was a green space, where she could see movement in the dim evening light. Squinting, she could make out two shadowed forms moving toward the riverbank.

"You will. Everyone finds it hard to refuse my offers. Isn't that right, Louis?" He laughed and patted the ship's captain on the shoulder. LeVoleur's voice drew her attention back to the conversation and to the Captain.

His lips compressed as he gave the mob boss a short nod.

"So long as we can all work harmoniously together, we can make a great profit together."

The corners of Captain Louis' mouth drew down further.

"It's not very...homey on board, is it? I tend to like my creature comforts."

"Ah, this way toward the personal quarters. I did my research before acquiring this vessel. I wanted to be sure it was suitable to our needs." He held a hand out, directing her toward the door out of the navigation room. As soon as he turned toward the door, Raya saw the captain and the pilot sag a little.

She could see why LeVoleur was eager to have her come and spy aboard the ship. At least some of the crew didn't appear to be committed.

The private quarters were as basic as she'd expected, fancied up with some expensive towels and bed linens. Her finger traced a hotel logo embroidered into the edge of the pillow case.

"Charming little space."

"Ah, see, Francois, I knew the towels would do the trick."

He pointed out key rooms and their functions as they worked their way back down to the deck level, then he led her down even further into the cavernous cargo holds. Most were filled with raw materials from the Great Lakes. There were a few containers here and there tucked away at the back, set apart from everything else.

This ship was set up much like the others she'd infiltrated. Human cargo would be in those containers.

"Tell me, what is it you think I can do here? You clearly have plenty of security."

"A man can never be too careful. Consider your role as security for my security. A fail safe." He smiled.

"I'm not interested just now. I have several jobs lined up already."

LeVoleur's smile faltered. "You're turning down my offer?"

"As I said, I have other work I'm committed to. Other contracts that deserve my attention, as much as yours did."

"You know, I was surprised to find out that my little problem turned out to be a relative of yours. I really was not expecting that." He held up a finger, shaking it. "And I bet you weren't either," he said, turning toward her.

She froze, waiting for his next words. How did he know? Had Chuck told him to save himself?

He went on. "I was surprised that you would just hand him over to me like that. Very surprised. And incredibly impressed."

Icy tension pierced the muscles of her shoulders.

"So committed. Dedicated to your reputation. Flawless. Cold." He moved closer. "Ruthless." His voice rasped and his eyes flashed as he approached her.

She said nothing, waiting.

"Still. I imagine it couldn't have been easy. Not knowing what my intentions were for your brother. So fascinating to learn this. Fascinating. I still find it hard to believe."

Her chin notched upward.

"Made it easier to find out more about *you* though. Broke through that thick veneer of mystery. Less a ghost and more a—p*erson*. The last living member of your family. The information almost humanized you. But, you're not human. Are you?"

She held his gaze when he looked at her.

"*We* are more than them." His fingertips drifted up her arm, his pupils dilating.

She suppressed the overwhelming shudder that threatened to wrack her body.

Disappointment pulled at his features at her lack of response. His hand dropped. "Would you like him back, as part of our contract? After I've questioned him, of course. I have to know what he knows. And backtrack where he's been and who he might have talked to, etcetera."

He was testing her. She had to tread carefully. If she showed interest in Dominique's safety, he would question her motivation. If she was completely disinterested, he might kill him as she expected he would anyway.

"What would I do with him? Especially if you insist on having me work here."

"He could keep you company." He shrugged. "A familiar face among strangers. Until you get to know me better. I'd certainly like to get to know you much, much better." His lascivious eyes swept her.

She was used to it. It was expected. She still didn't fucking like it when a man looked at her like she was something to satisfy his whim.

No matter that her reputation was of a hardened mercenary, it always came to this.

In the end, after a little time together, it came down to the fact that she was little more than a piece of ass. Another conquest to be added to the trophy wall, like a hillbilly lording over his man-cave shed.

The look she gave him dared him to touch her again. LeVoleur read her expression and stepped back a pace, turning away from her.

"And what would this *company* cost me, from the price you have yet to offer, so I can decide if any of it is worth my time? Working aboard the confines of a ship is of little interest to me."

"Hmmm, hard bargain. I like it. Shall we go up?" He waved his hand to ascend back up to deck level where she could see Dominique and Chuck were being held amid several armed mob thugs.

Her heart hammered in her chest. She turned to LeVoleur, frowning. "You spent an awful lot of money to hire me for the enormous effort to break your nephew out of prison and retrieve his lover for you."

"Yes."

"And, just like that, you're going to offer him to me for company aboard your ship."

"Yes."

"What would you have done with him, had he not been a relation of mine?"

"As I said. I needed to know what he knows. What he has seen. Then put him right back where he belongs. I was expected to deliver a certain amount of goods. Well, I'm sure you know how it is when you're hired to do something and come up short." His smile didn't meet his eyes.

He's going to sell him. Pick up like the last decade hadn't happened.

"Can't say that I do."

His smile faltered.

"I am curious though, why such the effort now? I mean, Dominique went missing years ago. Seems rather...late."

"Hmm, yes." LeVoleur walked up to Chuck and studied his defiant face. "Francois saw you with your lover, here." He sniffed as his gaze slid to Dominique. "A face like that, all those freckles and red hair, is very memorable. I sent you to the west coast job to get you away long enough for us to find him ourselves. My men came up empty. Then you got yourself arrested." He sighed. "At least you didn't land in a GPSA prison. Now that would have been challenging."

Impossible, more like.

"Anyway, my investors heard of your imprisonment, and knowing what you do about the business, they were concerned. So, I thought it best to round everyone up and deal with your mess, Charles."

"He doesn't know anything. He never did." Chuck said.

"Hmm. I'm disappointed you think me so naive to believe that. No, I'm sure he knows probably as much as you do."

Chuck opened his mouth to speak.

"Don't," LeVoleur snapped, "Don't you dare stoop to begging," he said, switching to French, "My family—my blood—never begs."

Another vehicle arrived, rolling to a stop beside the other SUVs by the access bridge.

LeVoleur turned to Raya. "If you don't want him as part of your contract, he will be put back into circulation. I mean to recover my money, one way or another," he said the last to Chuck, whose face reddened.

Dominique blanched.

Before Raya could answer, he went to meet the new arrivals. No one on the deck of the ship moved.

All of LeVoleur's men were armed. Some could be shifters, but she didn't know how many, or which ones.

"Welcome, welcome!" LeVoleur's superfluous greeting was a sign that he was becoming agitated.

This was important to him.

She turned her attention to the new arrivals approaching. All white-haired older men with impeccable appearances and a haughty tilt of their noses. She recognized two. Her mind worked to recall where she'd seen them before.

"Thank you for coming all this way. I do hope you've enjoyed touring the region before our meeting."

"Yes, Jean-Guy, very quaint. Good to see you again," one said; an older man with deep scowl lines, drooping jowls, and an east coast accent.

Investors?

As she struggled to place the other faces, Raya's body tingled. The undeniable sensation of Ian's magic rippling against her essence pulled her attention toward the river.

She moved toward the starboard side of the ship. Everyone's attention was on LeVoleur as he escorted his visitors to tour the ship as he'd done with her.

Seemingly forgotten, she inched her way into the shadows. When Dom turned to look for her, she held up a finger and dispersed.

IAN STRIPPED, STUFFED HIS clothes into the waterproof bag Ana had given him, and slipped into the inky water. As soon as he was out far enough, he swam close to the ship, keeping to the shadows.

Carson followed, running along the bank, close to the underbrush to stay out of sight of the floodlights with mounted cameras. He was a better shot with a gun, so Ian decided to go beast for now. If he could get close enough, he might be able to hear what was going on. Keeping to the shadows, he glanced around the river to ensure there weren't any observers before sinking below the surface to shift.

The water rippled around him as his body stretched; muscle, bone and sinew morphed. The river water displaced, making room for his mass as he grew, next to the ship.

Waiting for his sensitive hearing to adjust to the ambient sounds, Ian listened next to the hull of the ship. Crew called to one another as they worked. Cargo was being moved from one section to another. And the low murmur of other voices. Many voices, weak and full of despair. Off at the far end of the ship, he could hear someone crying.

Dear Goddess.

Yet another bolt of the reality of Raya's life over these last several years slid home.

He lifted his head, mindful to keep it below the line of the deck.

Then he felt Raya's magic.

"What the hell are you doing here in your beast, Ian? You can be seen by anyone." Her voice scathed him.

He didn't bother turning, knowing he wouldn't be able to see, nor answer her, in his present form.

She huffed. "There are visitors here. They look like investors. LeVoleur wants me to play babysitter aboard this ship while it's on route to pass off the human cargo. The ship is leaving tonight."

A low growl rumbled through his chest.

"I'm not going if I can help it." She said. "Stay out of sight, I'm going to see what else I can find out."

Her presence floated away like a fading melody.

Ian sank to his human state as he returned to Carson. Putting Ana's earpiece back on, he relayed what Raya told him to Carson's team.

Carson nodded. "Ana, call Jack, he'll need to reach out to his contacts with local law enforcement."

Ana's voice sounded in his ear. "Already done. His GPSA agent embedded with them is standing by with the Coast Guard. And Teddy's on his way."

"Teddy! Good, catch them up."

"Copy."

"We're going to see if we can get on that boat," Carson said to Ian.

"I'm positioned close to the vehicles," Lirikai said through the earpiece.

"Hold."

"Copy."

"Want a ride?" Ian said to Carson.

Carson grinned as Ian handed him his bag of clothes. Shifting back into his beast, he stretched his tail out so Carson could run up the length of his spine.

Sliding through the water back toward the ship, Ian eased alongside it then positioned himself so that, after a quick glance for guards, Carson could climb over the rail of the deck. He quickly found a lifesaver hanging nearby and tossed it over. Ian again reclaimed his human form and scrambled up the rope.

Taking the bag of clothes from Carson, he dressed before sneaking around the back, trying to get the holster Ana had given him in place.

RAYA LEFT IAN'S SIDE, and floated her way into the ship, looking for LeVoleur and his business partners.

The ship was leaving tonight, he'd said back at the hotel. She had to do this now, before it started navigating the treacherous waters of the river toward the gulf.

She found the investors in the cargo hold, grouped around an open container with an armed guard. LeVoleur was off to the side, talking to Francois.

She hadn't been wrong.

There were several dozen people in the one container, as she'd expected. Judging by the stink of the steel box, they'd been in there awhile already.

She floated closer to LeVoleur.

"Thanks to your loyalty, I've got Charles back where I can keep an eye on him. Stupid that he thought he could get away with deceiving me like that. Disappointing. I was preparing him to take my place. No matter. I will deal with him, and in the meantime, you will continue to work in his position until he can see reason."

"Yes, sir." Francois grinned, looking pleased with himself. "And the other one?"

"If the Ashray doesn't want him as part of her contract, throw him in with the others. If she does, she can have him until the ship makes contact at sea. *Then* he can go with the others." He sneered. "I don't want him back in this hemisphere again."

"If she objects?"

LeVoleur swept Francois with his gaze and grinned. "You can have her."

Francois frowned. "Yes, sir." He swallowed hard but nodded.

Good. He's afraid of me.

Raya moved back out toward the deck, floating toward Chuck and Dom.

"Be ready for anything." She whispered, making them both jump.

Sliding into the shadows, she rematerialized, strolling with her hands clasped behind her back as though she'd been touring the deck all this time.

Moments later, LeVoleur reappeared with his visitors, pulling her attention to their faces again. Where had she seen those two before?

The first clicked. She'd seen the more austere of the two at one of LeVoleur's meetings she'd spied on years ago, before she'd made contact with the underworld. The other...

The group were almost to the bridge to disembark from the ship. They stopped to wait their turn and the last in the line, the one that Raya couldn't figure out where she'd seen him before turned, noticing her looking at him.

Being the only female on board, she stood out.

His attention honed in on her, eyes widening as he recognized her at the same time she recalled how she knew him too.

Jones.

One of the liaisons between the Federal government and the *Organization*. They'd crossed paths, once, when she had been summoned for a debriefing after a successful mission.

Mother. Fucker.

TWENTY-FIVE

RAISED VOICES DREW IAN's attention toward the open deck. Inching forward from his position at the stern of the ship, the lit deck eased into view.

Raya stood alone in the middle, guards spread out around her. LeVoleur strode toward Chuck Meduse and Raya's brother, Dominique. Several older men in suits were in the process of descending to the pier. The last of the line was turned, pointing at Raya.

His indignant shouts carried across the deck of the ship. "This project is compromised. That woman is an international agent, LeVoleur, and I suggest you get rid of her."

LeVoleur spun, wide-eyed, in Raya's direction.

Fuck. This wasn't good.

He recalled her concerns at the cabin on the matter of a corrupt link somewhere between GPSA and her Organization.

"Shit." Carson's voice sounded in the earpiece. "Shit."

"What is it?" Ana said.

"Deputy Director Jones, in the chain of command. Well above my pay grade. Somewhere above Kane. This isn't good."

"Oh, this isn't good at all." Ana's voice was quiet.

"I'll take care of him." Lirikai said.

"Don't let those men leave the port, Lirikai. And don't eat them either. We need them."

"You know the scent of all this corruption is making me salivate."

"Copy?"

"Copy," she answered, with a heavy sigh.

LeVoleur was talking, voice too low to hear. He now stood in front of Raya, talking down at her, clearly enraged.

She shook her head.

LeVoleur spun back toward the older man.

"I'll goddamned well do it myself." The old man shouted, as he pulled a gun from inside his blazer and leveled it at Raya. She dematerialized as a shot resounded. The bullet disappeared into the darkness over the water.

She rematerialized with her forearm across his throat, the point of her knife pricking the sagging flesh below his ear.

"That...was rude," she said as he struggled to free himself from her grip.

"Release him," LeVoleur commanded.

"He shot at me," Raya said.

"I don't care, I told you to release him."

Raya didn't move.

In light of her defiance, LeVoleur drew a gun of his own and aimed it at Dominique.

"That man is an integral part of my operations. Let him go."

After a moment, he cocked the gun.

"If you fire that gun, I will slit your throat, LeVoleur."

His eyes widened, then he grinned. "Not so removed from your little brother after all, are you?" Despite his bravado, his aim faltered.

He'd just threatened the Ashray. And she was having none of it.

Pride swelled Ian's heart.

The old man grunted as blood trickled below the tip of Raya's blade toward his crisp collar.

"Hold." Carson's voice was soft through the earpiece.

"If that kid dies..." Ian ground out through his teeth.

"LeVoleur doesn't have any reason to kill him. He can't sell a dead man."

Ian was skeptical.

Movement pulled Ian's attention to a large figure moving in from the side. It was one of the neck-less goons from that morning and he was drawing a gun.

"Dom!" Raya yelled, having seen him at the same time Ian had.

The large man cocked the gun and fired in the same moment Chuck Meduse slid in front of Dominique, hand outstretched. A long clear cord whipped out of what should have been Meduse's hand, wrapping around the man's throat with a snap as his own body jerked back into Dominique with a grunt.

"Chuck!" Dominique yelled.

They both dropped to the deck, and chaos erupted.

The shooter also dropped to the ground, desperately clutching at the translucent cord wrapped around his throat, his face turning first red, then purple. The cord released him, retracting back into Chuck's limb. His face was pale as blood oozed from his chest.

More thugs moved toward Chuck and Dom. Raya's elbow came down on the old man's head, knocking him unconscious.

LeVoleur was bellowing.

Raya ran toward Dom, telling him to run. Seeing the turn of Raya's priorities, LeVoleur aimed his gun and fired at her. She dissipated and rematerialized next to a couple of guards, taking them down seconds before LeVoleur's bullets passed through the vacated space, some hitting his own men.

Several of the guards shifted.

The old men that were still conscious ran for their guarded vehicles, where Lirikai met them with horrific extended teeth. Ana aimed a Taser and her gun at them.

Raya was occupied evading guards. Carson had moved in and was fighting hand to hand with another.

Someone ran toward Ian with a long steel rod. He engaged the goon, while still trying to keep an eye on Dominique. He'd promised to keep him safe.

LeVoleur turned, wild-eyed, on Dominique, who still cradled Chuck as he bled.

"You! All this for you, you little piece of shit!" He advanced, gun drawn. "Charles, you stupid fuck. You ruined my legacy, the one you were meant to take over. For what?"

"I didn't want it, uncle," Chuck said, chest heaving with pain.

Raya cried out as she took a hit, her attention on her brother as LeVoleur advanced.

Ian sent the guy he'd been fighting sailing over the edge of the ship with a heavy splash, then ran toward Dominique and LeVoleur, trying to pull Ana's gun from its holster as he moved his body into the space between them. He aimed the gun at LeVoleur.

"I need him alive!" Raya shouted as she brought down a tiger shifter, then turned as another one of LeVoleur's men ran toward her.

A muscular figure with shoulder length blond hair jumped into the fray, shifting into a badger, attacking the man before he reached Raya. A panther followed close behind, launching for the neck of another one of the mob goons.

As LeVoleur swung his gun toward Ian, Raya moved in, her arms around LeVoleur as she'd done with the old man, knife at his throat.

LeVoleur fired his gun.

Pain exploded in Ian's chest as he knocked the gun loose, sending it clattering across the deck.

"Ian!" Raya screamed, wide eyes on the blood blooming on his chest. Fury transformed her features into a menacing mask.

Sirens wailed in the distance, echoing off the city buildings.

Ian managed to remain standing; the gun he pointed at LeVoleur wavered.

LeVoleur laughed at him, despite Raya's knife pinned to his throat.

"You're not going to kill me." They were standing close to the edge of the ship.

His eyes darted toward the edge a second before he threw his head back into Raya's nose.

She held fast, knife digging deeper. Her hand shook as her eyes flicked back to Ian's wound.

"You're not worth the effort to keep you alive." She growled.

LeVoleur grimaced in pain.

"You destroy people's lives."

Blood began to trickle faster from LeVoleur's throat as Raya's knife sliced deeper.

"Raya, you said you needed him alive," Ian prompted, panting.

"I changed my mind. We have all the evidence we need on this ship, plus the investors, and Chuck."

"Charles is my nephew. He won't tell you anything."

"Are you sure about that?"

LeVoleur's eyes slid to Chuck. The first of the emergency responders had arrived and were surrounding the port. Dominique was supporting Chuck as they carefully made their way off the ship.

The pain in Ian's chest grew. He needed to shift to dislodge the bullet if it was still in his flesh.

Carson finished handcuffing the last of the criminals he'd brought down and had just turned his attention to LeVoleur. "You're done. Let's go."

The sound of electricity crackled in the space in front of Ian. Raya screamed as the air around LeVoleur turned white-blue with ozone. Raya held tight, arms locked around LeVoleur.

The electricity was coming from LeVoleur and growing brighter.

Water and electricity didn't mix, and Raya was a creature made of water.

"Raya!" Ian bellowed, surging forward. It was too late.

LeVoleur forced Raya off balance, sending them both over the edge of the ship into the river.

Ian went in after them.

The water was alive, shocking him as soon as he touched it. The pain was worse than the bullet wound.

Raya.

Ian shifted.

He'd never experienced anything so excruciating as he did in those seconds between man and beast.

Once his beast was solidified, his thick hide dampened the effects of the electricity.

Raya hadn't let go. She was fading as she held onto the biggest electric eel Ian had ever seen. And it was still sending out waves of electricity in an effort to dislodge her grip.

With a final surge of a blue-white filament, Raya let go, her knife sinking to the bottom of the river as she floated free of LeVoleur.

Ian's brain fogged with panic at seeing her limp form.

He couldn't lose her now. He also couldn't let her efforts be for nothing.

Reason wriggled into his brain. Her magic wouldn't let her drown.

LeVoleur writhed through the water away from Ian and Raya.

With a growl, Ian's jaws snapped. Then again as he stretched his long neck forward, his teeth sinking into the eel, trapping it. Raising his head out of the water, he sent it flying up onto the deck of the ship before plunging back below the surface.

He aligned himself so that his neck slipped under Raya's inert form. As soon as he was sure her body was balanced, he carefully lifted her out of the water, where Carson was close by to help pull her onto the deck.

He dropped back into the river one last time to retrieve his clothes and shoes that had drifted loose during his shift and slipped them back on. He swam to the flotation device Carson had used to help him up onto the deck before and moments later he was at Raya's side. She was still unconscious. Dropping to his knees, he pressed his ear to her chest.

"She started breathing as soon as you got her out of the water." Carson told him.

He was sure she wouldn't have drowned in the water. There was no telling what that kind of electric charge would do to her, though, and he hadn't wanted to risk leaving her there any longer than necessary.

He listened carefully. Her heartbeat was faint and irregular, but it was still beating.

LeVoleur lay naked and bleeding from the wounds Ian had inflicted with his teeth. Lirikai loomed over him.

"He's not going anywhere." Carson said. "Are you okay, Ian?"

"Yes, shifting released the bullet and triggered the healing process."

Carson nodded. "Good, I'd hoped so. Getting shot sucks."

"Especially in the ass," Ana said, striding toward them. "Teddy's here."

Carson nodded. "I saw him. Never been so happy to see a badger in my life."

Ian peered into Raya's pale face, whispering her name.

Her eyes fluttered open and Ian's heart cracked with relief.

Her hand wavered toward him, landing on his cheek. "Have I ever told you how much I love your accent?"

"Not in a long, long while." He answered, laying it on thick.

She smiled.

Carson clapped him on the shoulder and moved back to where LeVoleur was. Ana went with him.

"Dominique?"

"He's okay."

Her eyes closed. When she re-opened them, they were full of tears. "I found him, Ian."

"Aye, you did, love."

She quickly blinked away the tears. "I feel like shit."

"Can you stand?"

She nodded. He helped her up and supported her for a few moments as she got her balance. "I'll be okay. I want to see him."

He smiled at her and kissed her forehead.

TWENTY-SIX

RAYA LOOKED UP FROM where she was seated next to Dominique, who held Chuck's hand as he lay on a gurney just outside of an ambulance.

Ian appeared before her.

The port was crowded with emergency vehicles, jammed into the spaces between shipping containers. Firetrucks, police cruisers and ambulances were barriers to enclose the scene. Coast Guard boats bobbed around the ship, so escapees could be retrieved from the water. Port employees, ship workers and criminals were being assessed and shuffled off for further processing.

"Carson is going to take Chuck and Dominique into GPSA's direct custody. Maeda and Kane are going to take over from here. You're expected to meet with them, too."

"Where is LeVoleur?" Raya asked, glancing around the red and blue lit chaos.

"Secured in an ambulance. Still breathing."

"So am I, thanks to you," Dominique said, reaching over to him, hand outstretched. "Thanks."

Ian shook it. "It's good to see you again."

Dominique nodded. "Good to be seen." He glanced at Raya with an awkward smile. "We have a lot of catching up to do."

"Aye, we do," Ian said, turning his gaze to Raya.

She looked from one to the other and laughed, shaking her head. "And we will." She reached out and squeezed Dom's hand.

"Time to go," Agent Perenga said from behind Raya. She turned to see him looking from Dom to Chuck. "We have a very long night ahead of us." He watched as Chuck's gurney was loaded into the ambulance.

Dominique tugged on Raya's hand, pulling her into a hug. "I'm okay, Raya. I'll be fine."

She hugged him so hard he wheezed, but he didn't complain. He returned the strength of it equally, his cheek resting on her head.

"I love you, little brother."

"I know you do, and I love you, too." He released her, glancing from Ian to Raya. "You really need to live for yourself. No matter what happens after tonight. I will be okay." He kissed her forehead and turned to take his place at Chuck's side in the ambulance.

Agent Perenga spoke briefly to the EMS driver then returned to Raya and Ian.

"What will happen to them?"

He shrugged. "The board of inquiry will assess them, see how cooperative they are, or aren't, and go from there."

Raya nodded, accepting this.

"This case just gets deeper and wider," he said to Ian.

"You have no idea," Raya said.

"I may, a little. Analiese told me about what she saw when she touched your hand. Sounds to me like we have an awful lot of work to do."

"Yes, we do." She looked up to Ian, seeing him study her face. "I'm not done yet." She said.

Ian slipped his fingers between hers, pulling her hand to his lips. "*We*...are not done yet."

She smiled as her heart fluttered at the look in his eyes.

"Teddy and the local GPSA agent, Pia Jensen, are waiting to talk to me. I'll see you both later," Agent Perenga said, giving Ian's shoulder a hearty clap.

RAYA OPENED HER EYES to see the early morning sunlight bathing Ian's sleeping face.

Her heart swelled as she stared at the illuminated angle of his jaw as the light caught on the new stubble, then at his lips, relaxed in sleep. She traced the tip of her thumb over a thick brow.

A moment later, she rolled away and rose from the bed, reaching for her discarded silk nightgown and wrap. Tying the belt, she stepped out onto the open terrace and drank in the sight of the loch below the cottage.

Ian's birthplace.

A fine morning mist lingered over the loch, which stretched out of sight in either direction. Wandering out further, her hands clasped the iron rail as the sun burned off last of the fog and made the water glitter like crystal shards.

She drew a deep breath, savoring it.

Home.

Ian had gone with her to pay her respects at her parents' grave site in Aberdeen before they drove to Inverness, where they were to spend the next couple of weeks.

The *Organization* had been satisfied with their procurement of LeVoleur and the shipload of victims. The investor that had tried to shoot her had also been taken into custody. The *Organization*, the government and GPSA were launching a deep investigation into his activities and connections.

While LeVoleur maintained his silence, Chuck gave the GPSA and the *Organization* everything they needed.

It appeared he did indeed want a life free of his uncle's criminal world. He and Dominique wouldn't be able to go back to Montreal. They'd have to make a new life elsewhere. And all the money she'd made as The Ashray was going to help them do just that-after she replaced agent Ortega's shoes.

Raya felt the warmth of Ian's body before his hands slid around her. She shivered, knowing she'd never get too used to the sensation of his touch.

"Want to go for a swim later?" His brogue was thick next to her ear. Her nipples pebbled.

"Maybe." A smile played at her lips. "Think any tourists will be around?"

"We can look for them."

She giggled.

She felt his chest rise against her back as he drew a deep breath. "Good to be home?"

"Aye. I shouldn't have stayed away so damned long. I was foolish." He turned her to face him. "Foolish about so many things."

Her fingers drifted over his cheek and jaw. He kissed her fingertips.

"I've caused us to lose so much time."

She shrugged. "We can look at it that way, I suppose. Maybe we needed it, Ian. Maybe we both needed that time to step up to the next level of who we are. Besides, the reunion has been incredible." She grinned, rubbing her body against his.

He hardened against her belly. "If we keep this up, I willnae be able to walk."

"We aren't going anywhere for a while." She whispered.

Ian's eyes were locked on her face.

She shivered at the intensity of his gaze.

"I love you so much, Raya. I nearly died when I thought I'd lost you again."

"Ian." Her voice was so very soft. "It will happen one day. Hopefully a very long time from now, but it will. And with the work I do..."

"I'll be there with you, Raya."

"To protect me. As much as you can."

"Will you let me?"

"Sometimes. Will you let me protect you, too?"

He smiled. "Sometimes."

"Then we have an agreement."

He nodded.

She slid her hand into the front of his lounge pants, wrapping her fingers around him.

Ian's hands pushed her gown up, then lifted her so that her bottom rested on the railing.

"Now," Her voice dropped, turning husky. "Talk to me in that dirty brogue of yours, and I'll think about letting you in."

He lowered his mouth next to her ear, where his lips grazed the shell. "I'm going to make you scones for breakfast, love." He bit her earlobe. "With fresh butter."

Raya wrapped her legs around his hips and guided him to her entrance. She moaned as he slid home.

This was turning out to be a wonderful lakeside vacation indeed, and beautiful start to a second chance with the love of her life.

Analiese Ortega's story continues in *Polestar*, Book #3 of the GPSA: Aquatic Investigations...

Carson & Lirikai   Ian & Raya   Magnus & Ana   Pia & Renni

The Global Paranormal Security Agency

JodiKendrick.com

Teddy's story is in 'Defending Her Honey Badger' by Renee Hewett!

Thank You!

Dear Reader,

Thank you so much for taking the time to read *Surfacing*. If you enjoyed it, please consider leaving a review on your favourite platform.

For free downloads, to join my newsletter and browse my growing library for more books with *Romance, Adventure and Passion*, visit **JodiKendrick.com**

-Jodi

ABOUT JODI KENDRICK

Jodi Kendrick lives in Eastern Ontario Canada with her *Favourite Person* and chompy furbaby, while their adult children explore the wider world.

As a romance author, she writes in paranormal, fantasy, steampunk & gaslamp subgenres, and sometimes delves into urban fantasy and paranormal women's fiction. Her characters are often quirky, sometimes cranky, but they all woman-up and get the job done while their partners ensure they survive with all their bits and bobs attached.

A history enthusiast and word dabbler most of her life, she enjoys exploring 'beyond-the-everyday' and the 'time-before-now', discovering relationship threads weaving individuals through time and place. She's rarely seen without flashy notebooks and colourful pens.

Follow Jodi on Social Media:

Dragon Island
Dragon Heat

Enchanted Ardor
Wish

EveL Worlds : FUCN'A
Tough Nut
Diamond in the Ruff
Honeyed Nut
Gorilla in the Hiss
FUCN'A Collection One
Pedigree Collection

Finely Aged
Dragon Steel

Global Paranormal
Security Agency

Awakened
Surfacing
Polestar
Aquatic Investigations
Prowler

The Kindred Chronicles

Healer
Mercenary

The Soaring Dragon Chronicles
Return Flight
Changeling